"Put that toy away," Tracewski said, halting in front of Caesar. "Frank wouldn't like that. We got a deal. Kill me, and you kill the deal." He lifted the blue suitcase and patted it affectionately. "I got the goodies right here."

Caesar lowered the .22.

"Now go in and tell Frank I'm ready to deal." The repo man turned his back on Caesar and headed for the restaurant. For just a crazy minute, Caesar considered coldcocking the creep and dragging him to Frank's apartment—but Tracewski looked too heavy for that.

After Tracewski had gone into the restaurant, Caesar hurried around back to Frank's deck. Frank was relaxing in a lounge chair, drink in hand.

"You find him?" he asked when he saw Caesar.

"I found him. He's downstairs in the restaurant. He has the stuff. He says he's ready to deal."

"I don't believe it," Frank said, getting to his feet. Just then, a black limousine crunched to a halt in the lot below the deck. Frank peered over the deck's railing. He did not have to be told who was sitting in the back seat.

"Get inside, Caesar," Frank said. "We got ourselves a visitor. Come all the way from Jersey . . ."

BODY PARTS

BILL KNOTT

Smp
ST. MARTIN'S PAPERBACKS

St. Martin's Paperbacks titles are available at quantity discounts for sales promotions, premiums or fund raising. Special books or book excerpts can also be created to fit specific needs. For information write to special sales manager, St. Martin's Press, 175 Fifth Avenue, New York, N.Y. 10010.

BODY PARTS

Copyright © 1991 by Bill Knott.

All rights reserved. No part of this book may be used or reproduced in any manner whatsoever without written permission except in the case of brief quotations embodied in critical articles or reviews. For information address St. Martin's Press, 175 Fifth Avenue, New York, N.Y. 10010.

ISBN: 0-312-92422-4

Printed in the United States of America

St. Martin's Paperbacks edition/ February 1991

10 9 8 7 6 5 4 3 2 1

For Judy

CHAPTER 1

Jimmy Vasquez glanced at his watch as he drove the ramp truck into Hudson Creek. It was only four. He was early. Halfway down Main Street he hung a left onto Canal Street. Following the directions Skip had given him, he kept on toward the river, then turned right onto an unpaved muddy lane and found himself deep in white trash. Fat women in tank tops sat on tiny porches, arms crossed, porcine eyes peering at him as he drove past. Filthy, half-naked kids in shrieking packs cut across the road in front of him, a few brandishing realistic-looking plastic machine pistols. On rutted lawns and driveways, hulks of old cars and pickup trucks rusted. Packs of snarling curs roamed free. The sight of a pit bull straining on a chain nailed to a fence post turned his balls to ice.

He approached a small one-story frame house—asbestos green siding peeling from its walls, its front porch sagging. He slowed, glanced at the driveway, saw no sign of Mary Lou Dobbs's Lamborghini, and drove on past. He kept going until he reached a gravel roadway, cut onto an alley which took him back to the town's main drag. Shifting clumsily, he turned onto it and drove back out of town, swinging into the Lands End Motel just outside of town.

He parked the ramp truck there and walked back into Hudson Creek to the town's one-story cinderblock police station. He entered and found himself in a vestibule the size of a walk-in closet, a sliding glass window on his right. A dough-faced woman cop slid aside the glass partition and stopped chewing her gum long enough to ask if she could help him.

"I want to see the captain."

"Captain Wendover?"

"If that's his name."

"What's the nature of your business with the captain?"

He handed the company card to her. "I'm in town to pick up a car."

She glanced at the card. "Repossession?"

"Yeah. That's what it's called."

She looked at him like he'd just farted and handed the card back. "Have you got the car outside?"

BODY PARTS

"No. I'll pick it up later tonight. Just checkin' in early so there won't be no trouble."

Her eyes gleamed with undisguised hostility. "There'll be no trouble, long as you come in to see us after you pick it up."

"I know the procedure. This ain't the first one I recovered."

"You got your dealer plates?"

"Yeah, and my ramp truck is parked down the road at the motel." He glanced past her. "Maybe I better report to the captain," he told her. "While I'm here."

"Captain's not here now. You come in later tonight, it'll be Sergeant Booker you'll have to see."

She slid the window shut and picked up a clipboard. He left the station and paused on the sidewalk in front of it, vaguely pissed, wishing he could have left the lady cop with a fat lip. But he told himself not to get all bent out of shape. By this time he should be used to local cops dumping on him. No one liked a repo man.

He shifted his feet and looked up and down the business district. What a dipshit of a place. Not even a Burger King, for Christ sake, just a crummy diner on a corner at the other end of town. He crossed the street and was passing the drugstore when, wouldn't you know it, the white Lamborghini pulled up. Grinning at his luck, he paused to watch Mary Lou Dobbs get out of the car.

Jesus Christ, he thought, when she stood back to slam the loony gull wing door shut. What a shame to take anything back from this baby.

3

Bill Knott

Perfect face. High cheekbones. Green eyes highlighted by green eyeliner. Outthrust, pouty lips. Jugs straining against a red, bare-midriff tank top. Black cropped pants snug enough so her pudenda and hip bones stood out in bold relief. Gold hoop earrings gleamed against the tousled, lush fall of her crimped, shoulder-length blond hair. When she stepped up onto the sidewalk beside him, he saw the fire-engine red pumps and black mesh stockings. She was a working girl, no doubt about it, and this was all advertisement. Which went a long way to explaining the Lamborghini.

As she clicked across the sidewalk she turned her head and caught him looking at her. She paused. Her smile was dazzling, like she was practicing on him.

"Do I know you?" she asked.

"I don't know," he said. *"Do* you?"

She shook her head. "You ski?"

"No, and I don't ice skate, either."

She looked at his shoulders. "You must work out."

He didn't, but he wasn't going to tell her that.

"You new in town?"

"You could say that."

Her tongue moistened her lips, slowly. He began to perspire as his eyes took her all in. There wasn't much he had to imagine.

"Take a good look," she told him, "but that's all you get. I don't think you can afford me."

"Not so, lady. I already owe you a bundle."

She swept on past him into the drugstore. He wanted to follow her in and make a move on her, but he remembered why he was up here in the first place

BODY PARTS

and continued on down the street to the diner. Today he would be a good boy. Besides, she was right. He couldn't afford her.

But she couldn't afford that Lamborghini, either.

Like a pearl on black velvet, the Lamborghini glowed in the moonlight—only the black velvet happened to be a littered driveway. He didn't need a slim jim to open the car door; she hadn't locked it, and besides, he had the keys. As he slipped in behind the wheel and inserted the key in the ignition switch, a whiff of dimestore perfume caused him to turn his head. Mary Lou Dobbs was leaning over, peering into the car.

"Oh," she said, recognizing him. "It's you."

He turned on the motor.

"Yeah. Surprise."

"You mean you're going to steal my car?"

"Not steal it, repossess it."

He had learned from Skip that once you get behind the wheel, shag ass. Don't discuss nothin'. He dropped his hand and shifted into reverse, but did not floor the accelerator.

Instead he said, "I can't afford you. You can't afford this car."

"But this is all a mistake! Honestly! It's all paid for!"

"Come on. Where would you get enough for a car like this?"

"It's a gift."

Bill Knott

Gazing at her knockers, he could believe it.

"Then you better go see your boyfriend," he told her. "Looks like he screwed up on the payments."

"Please! Just give me time to prove it. The car's all paid for!"

"You got the title, a bill of sale?"

"Not here. But I can get it."

"Sorry."

He looked behind him to back out.

"Just give me a chance," she pleaded, leaning her head into the car so he wouldn't go anywhere. "Please."

He looked her over, aware that a crucial psychological moment had long since passed. Aware, too, that he wanted what she was offering. Her swollen tank top gave him a spectacular view of her cleft, and this close he could smell the sweaty heat of her body.

He took his foot off the accelerator.

"Maybe," he said, "you ain't too expensive for me after all."

Leaning all the way into the car, she kissed him on the lips, her tongue alive, her left hand closing about his crotch. When she pulled back, he took a second or two before he spoke up. He didn't want to sound like a kid.

"Get in," he told her. "My truck's at the motel. We can talk there. Maybe. I'm not promising nothin'."

She was around the car in an instant, jumping in beside him, her hand reaching over and squeezing his thigh as she pulled the door shut.

"I really do appreciate this," she told him.

BODY PARTS

As he backed out of the driveway, he could hear Skip's words of warning again. He had to admit it. Skip was right on target. He never should've let this dame start talking, and he never should've listened when she did. But not to worry. No way would he let her talk him out of taking this boat back. Of course that didn't mean he was obliged to put any obstacles in her path if the poor, unhappy dame wanted to use all her talents to convince him otherwise.

Naked as a plucked chicken, he lay spread-eagled on the bed, pleasantly drained. She'd sure as hell hauled his ashes. If he snapped the window shade, he'd likely go right up with it. He could hear her in the shower singing softly. A girl who loved her work.

As soon as she had entered the motel, she'd called her man. Jimmy had been in the shower through most of the conversation and hadn't heard all she'd told the poor son of a bitch, but when he came out of the bathroom, she assured him her friend had promised to bring her the car's title first thing in the morning. With some relish, her green eyes sparkling, she told Jimmy how she'd read her Daddy Warbucks the riot act, reminding him what trouble she could make for him if he didn't come up with that title. She must have something on him for sure. What it was, Jimmy had no idea, but he was perfectly willing to leave that part of it to her.

And she was more than willing to give a great part of herself to him. Between bouts she talked a lot, and he had found himself listening with growing interest. She'd been back from Miami for a week now and was dealing nose candy in Lake Placid. From the way it sounded, she had a steady string of flush customers, all of them working on a growing habit.

At the moment, then, with her singing in the shower, he was happily contemplating his radically altered future. His days of struggle and privation were behind him. No more dogs nipping at his ankles. No worry that he might have to return to McDonald's. His luck had changed. Mary Lou Dobbs had found Jimmy Vasquez to be the fuck of her life, and in sheer gratitude she was going to let him in on the action. When she told him how much they could clear and he had considered the perks she'd willingly provide for a man with his shoulders, he had not taken long to agree. And right now, gazing up at the ceiling, his arms crossed under his head, he could feel the elation at his prospects building within him.

Mary Lou appeared in the bathroom doorway, a towel draped over one shoulder, a hand brushing her damp hair back, her body glowing from the hot water. Without the eye shadow, and with her face scrubbed clean, she looked good enough to eat. She flicked the towel back into the bathroom.

"Come here," she said softly.

He left the bed and kissed her open mouth, then allowed his lips to brush past her wet nipples, down over the lush swell of her belly. He kept on. Her fingers tightening in his thick hair, she told him huskily that maybe they should return to the bed. Lifting her in his arms, he spun about and dumped her onto it. She uttered a squeal of delight and, reaching up, flung her arms around his neck and pulled him down onto her.

A loud, shuddering knock came at the door.

She froze under him.

"You in there, bitch?" came from the other side. The voice was harsh, brutal.

"Oh, Jesus!" she cried in a fierce whisper. "It's Moon! Don't answer!"

"Your boyfriend?"

"Don't let him in! Please!"

Jimmy heard two men talking, discussing what to do next. It didn't take them long to figure it out. The next knock was really a shattering blow. It sounded like they were using a sledgehammer. A door panel splintered and the door sagged open. Two men rushed into the room, the one in the lead the biggest, craziest-looking son of a bitch he had ever seen. He was carrying an ax and coming right for him.

Oh, Christ! This is it, Jimmy thought. He'd bought it. He wouldn't be spending all that loot now, and there'd be no more nookie . . . no more Mary Lou Dobbs . . .

He flung his arm up.

The ax sliced through his forearm and continued its downward sweep to smash through his right shoulder, severing his arm and brutally spinning him around. A second blow blotted out the vision on his left side. The last thing he saw before a red curtain descended was Mary Lou crouched in a corner, too terrified to scream.

CHAPTER 2

EARLIER THAT SAME DAY SKIP AND TROOPER TERRY LINDsay had finished dinner and were waiting for the waitress to notice and bring the check.

Terry lifted the napkin from her lap and folded it neatly on the table beside her plate. "Really, Skip, you needn't have acted so put upon. It's a *very* nice place."

"I didn't say it wasn't."

Disregarding regulations, and on the pretext of showing him the new blue-and-gold she'd been assigned, Terry had taken Skip for a ride to a lake a few miles north of Albany to look at a cabin she had discovered, one she had been certain was perfect for him.

"Right on the lake," she reminded him, "and just four rooms. So little to keep up. And that view! You'd love it there, Skip."

"You a trooper, Terry, or moonlighting for Century 21?"

"I just hate to think of you living at the Summit Lodge."

"You mean you don't like coming to see me in a motel? Maybe you got an image problem."

He despised this kind of put-down himself and was only kidding, but he hit too close to home and she bristled.

"You know that's not the reason."

"Hey. Take it easy. Just kidding."

They had pulled into this roadside restaurant a few minutes after six, and as Terry strode in ahead of Skip in her gray uniform—her flat-brimmed Stetson causing her to duck her head slightly, a .357 magnum in an open-toed flapped leather holster snugged against her slim waist—everyone in the place had gone quiet. And during the meal, diners kept stealing glances at them. The scrutiny didn't bother Skip any, and he knew Terry was unconcerned as well. She had grown accustomed to this sort of thing when she led her Cornell swim team four years back, the one that took so many golds at the summer Olympics. It was all that competitive swimming that gave her such impressive shoulders.

What many of these diners were wondering, Skip realized, was what a man in his condition would be doing with this statuesque state trooper. Closer to forty than thirty, Skip was a cross between the Genie of the Bottle and Kojak. A shambling bear of a man with a shiny, bald pate he usually kept covered with a snap-brim felt hat, he favored dark suits, shirt and tie, an overcoat when necessary, and black shoes highly polished. His father had once remarked that a man with unpolished shoes was an abject failure who was broadcasting this fact to the world.

"It really isn't, you know," she persisted.

"An image problem?"

"It isn't."

"I'm sorry I said that."

"It's not like you."

"What it is, you think I'm unsafe at the Summit Lodge. Someone's going to break in and glom my black and white TV set."

"Don't make fun of me, Skip. I don't like it." Her voice was sharp, but low enough so it would not carry. That's what he liked about Terry. Her control. There were other things he liked about her as well.

But this ongoing debate about where he lived or should live—this whole damn wasted afternoon, in fact—he didn't like one bit, and what pissed him off was that he hadn't seen it coming.

"You want me to assume the obligations of a real home," he said wearily. "That it?"

"You bastard. You know what I want you to assume."

"Look, Terry, I enjoy living at the motel. It's a very efficient place. Fresh linen every day; they handle all my calls and take messages if I'm not there. And there's a restaurant off the lobby that stays open till one and takes American Express."

"But you'd have so much more room in a place of your own."

"And property taxes and school taxes, and water taxes and sewage taxes, a leaky roof, a rotting porch, plumbing failures . . ."

"All *right*, Skip."

But he was off and running now. ". . . and a lawn to mow in the summer and sidewalks to shovel in the winter, a new paint job every five years, fuel bills, electricity bills, phone bills—and every goddamn agency of the state and federal government with their hands out. Terry, a homeowner in this state is the target of every tax ever dreamed up by a profligate government, federal, state, and local."

Her stare was icy. "You finished?"

"For now."

"Skip, don't you want another family?"

"Not when I consider what goes with it."

"Oh," she said tightly. "And what *does* go with it?"

Anyone who argues with a woman on this subject gets what he deserves, and what frosted him was that he should have known better. He waved the waitress over and asked for the check.

Then he smiled wearily at Terry. "Let's not do or say anything we might regret. Okay, Terry?"

He could tell she was already chiding herself for starting up again. Almost meekly, she said, "All right, Skip."

"Why not drop me off at the motel and get your

own car? Makes me nervous, that shiny new blue-and-gold sitting out there."

"All right."

"Then maybe you can come by later."

"I'd like that."

The waitress brought the check. He paid up and followed Terry from the restaurant. Inside the blue-and-gold he glanced over at her as she slipped in behind the wheel.

"I wonder if those diners thought I was your prisoner."

"Is that what *you* think?"

Oh, Christ, he thought as she drove off, gravel flying.

The phone woke Skip. Terry rolled away and buried her head under the pillow.

He lifted the receiver. "Who is it?"

"This is your brother. Buford. What's the matter? You got cotton in your ears?"

"What the hell time is it?"

"Six-thirty."

"Jesus, Buford."

"It's about that new kid."

"Jimmy?"

"Yeah. You sent him upstate after that Lamborghini, right?"

"To Hudson Creek."

"Well, I got a call from him last night, from the

Bill Knott

Lands End Motel, said he was on his way to pick up the car."

"So?"

"That was a little after eleven. And he ain't back here yet. I'm worried about the foolish bastard. He could've missed a curve and taken that ramp truck off the road. You know how wild that country is up there."

"Shit. That could be. He's a real hotshot."

"Go on up there. See what you can find out."

Skip wanted to argue. The kid might be pulling into the agency's holding compound that very minute. But he understood his brother's concern. Hell, he shared it.

"Okay, Buford. I'll call you soon as I find anything. If he comes rolling in while I'm up there, call that motel. I'll start there."

"All right."

Buford hung up. Skip dropped the phone onto the cradle and sat up on the edge of the bed. Terry propped herself up on her elbows.

"Trouble?"

"I wish I knew. Anyway, I got to move out. Go on back to sleep."

"You kidding? I'm wide awake now. What's this all about?"

"One of my repo men. Just a kid. He hasn't shown up, and he should've by now. Buford's afraid he might have gone off the road somewhere."

Skip flipped aside his blanket and padded on bare feet over to the small Sanyo refrigerator, pulled out a bucket of ice and the Jack Daniels. He built drinks for himself and Terry and tramped back to the bed, handing one to Terry.

She took it, her eyes somber. "Isn't it early for this?"

"I think I might need it."

"Do you know this young man very well?"

"He's just a punk kid, a product of the American public schools, but I like him well enough. I broke him in."

"I guess this isn't a good time for us to talk."

Skip took a good belt of his drink. She was goddamn right, it wasn't.

Terry reached out and took Skip's arm, holding it gently. "Do you know your pubic hair is getting gray?" It was a lame effort to cheer him up, he realized, and he was grateful for it.

He looked at her, grinning. "Just so long as it's not snow white."

"What's that about old bulls?"

"They like to feed on fresh grass."

"Is that what I am?"

"You are, and I am dutifully grateful."

She scooted back against the headboard and took a healthy belt of the Jack Daniels, then brushed her hair off her forehead.

"I'm real sorry about that beef in the restaurant, Skip."

"Forget it. No hard feelings."

He knew she wasn't going to forget it, that when she thought the time was ripe, she'd spring the whole enchilada on him again. She couldn't let it go. She was into communication, airing out the slightest

Bill Knott

disagreements and holding nothing back, searching out every possible motive, in the end expressing things better left unsaid.

"Do you mean that, Skip? No hard feelings?"

There she went, picking at the scab. He turned to look at her, not wanting any more of it.

"Of course I meant it. Now drop it, will you?"

"There's no need for you to snap at me."

With a weary groan, Skip finished his drink, got up and walked into the bathroom. When he finished his shower and stepped back into the room, vigorously rubbing himself dry with a bath towel, Terry was gone. But he didn't let it bother him. He wasn't thinking of her.

He was thinking of Jimmy Vasquez.

Less than a mile outside Hudson Creek, Skip caught sight of two blue-and-golds pulled up on the soft shoulder, one before and one beyond the Lands End Motel, with a third patrol car sitting in the motel's parking lot. All three troopers had left their roof beacons flashing, which accounted for the slowdown in the traffic as it flowed past the motel. Some drivers had already pulled onto the soft shoulder across from the motel to gawk. A trooper and a town cop were doing their best to keep the traffic moving.

Skip swung his Mazda into the motel parking lot. A rescue squad ambulance from Lake Placid was parked in front of the motel unit farthest from the motel office. Even before Skip braked his car, a town

BODY PARTS

cop left the unit and hurried across the macadam toward him, a trooper trailing behind.

They had made him so quickly, Skip realized, because of the decal on his car, one identical to that on the agency's ramp truck: the face of a Mohawk Indian glared out from inside a tire. MOHAWK ADJUSTMENT SERVICE was printed in bright red letters on the white sidewall, and under it the boast: IF IT ROLLS, FLOATS, OR FLIES, WE REPOSSESS—WE NEVER FAIL.

Skip got out of his car, one hand flying up to keep the wind from whipping off his hat. He shook hands first with the town cop who introduced himself as Sergeant Booker, then with the trooper, Captain Carmody, a tall, sandy-haired youth in his late twenties.

"Are you Skip Tracewski?" the town cop asked.

"Yeah, that's me."

"That was fast. I just got through talking to your brother on the phone. He said you were on your way up here."

"Slow down, Booker. What's this all about?"

"You sent a Jimmy Vasquez up here to repossess a vehicle?"

"I did."

"Good," said Carmody, pleased. "Then you'll be able to give us a positive ID."

Skip felt the color drain from his face. "Go slow here, will you? What's this all about? Where's Jimmy?"

"You don't know?" Booker said.

"Know what? My partner sent me up here to find

Vasquez. He's overdue, and we thought he might have gone off the road."

"He didn't go off the road," Booker told him gloomily. "You had your breakfast?"

"Haven't had time yet."

"Follow me."

Booker, a small fellow with round shoulders and a round ass, was apparently still shook up, and when Skip stepped into the motel unit a moment later, he understood why. The faint, sickly-sweet odor of blood hung in the air. Everywhere he looked—on the bed's coverlet, the walls, the carpet, the ceiling—deep mahogany stains of dried blood were visible.

Pete Moriarty stepped out of the bathroom, wiping his hands on a towel. The county coroner was an old acquaintance of Skip's. A thin man with sloping shoulders, he peered at Skip through gold-rimmed glasses.

"Well, well, Skip. Long time no see."

"There's a reason for that."

"I know. You repossess cars now."

"It's an honest job, Moriarty. No graft."

"Mr. Tracewski here will be making the positive ID," Captain Carmody told Moriarty.

With a shrug, Moriarty walked over to the bed and unzipped the body bag lying on it. Then he stepped back out of Skip's way. Skip wasn't sure what he was seeing at first, so he moved closer. The biggest item was a naked torso, minus the head and one arm, which had been sliced off at the shoulder. From the neck to the crotch great chunks of flesh had been chopped out, the wounds yawning up at him

BODY PARTS

like gaping mouths, revealing in their depths splintered bones, torn muscles, cartilege, nerves, internal organs. Alongside the torso the severed arm rested in two pieces. Jimmy's head sat beside it. One ear dangled loosely from the side of his crushed skull.

"That Vasquez?" Moriarty asked.

"How the hell am I supposed to know from this?"

"Take a guess."

"It's him."

Moriarty zipped the bag shut.

His mouth dry, Skip looked at Moriarty. "Where's the BCI boys?"

"They're on the way. I happen to live nearby, more's the pity."

Skip turned around and walked out of the motel into the bright morning sunlight. After seven years on the Albany police force, this was the first time his stomach had threatened to betray him. He had quit smoking a couple of years ago and was proud of it; but at that moment he very much wanted a cigarette.

Booker left with him. He looked about as bad as Skip felt. Carmody followed out behind them and waved to the two attendants leaning against the rescue squad ambulance. The trooper appeared to be holding up nicely.

"Guess you must be pretty shook up, Mr. Tracewski," he said. "Too bad you had to see that. We do appreciate your coming all the way up here to make the identification. I understand your business partner will be notifying the decedent's next of kin."

"That's my brother, Captain. And yes, I guess he'll be notifying the dead man's mother."

Bill Knott

"That's what I said, Mr. Tracewski. One more thing. The motel owner mentioned a white Lamborghini. I assume it's the vehicle your man was sent up here to repossess. Would you happen to have its tag number? The motel register gives only the plate number for your agency's truck parked over there. As soon as we get the Lamborghini's, we'll be able to put out an APB on it."

Skip gave the number to the captain, who dutifully took it down in his notebook.

"I don't think we'll have any trouble spotting this baby," he said, pleased.

"When you do, we'd appreciate a call."

"Why, of course, Mr. Tracewski."

"You got a cigarette?"

"I don't smoke," the captain informed Skip, frowning.

With a curt, no-nonsense nod to Booker, Carmody strode off to his waiting blue-and-gold. Their stretcher moving soundlessly on rubber wheels before them, the two rescue squad attendants disappeared into the motel and promptly came back out with Jimmy Vasquez's body parts resting on the stretcher. His jacket on, Moriarty stepped out of the motel, adjusted his tie, and with a casual wave to Skip, followed after the two attendants.

Skip looked at Booker. "What do you know about this Carmody?"

Booker grinned hollowly. "The captain? He's something, ain't he? A real tight-ass. He tells me he's in charge of the investigation."

"Where's your own chief?"

BODY PARTS

"Inside the motel office, quizzing the owner."

"He the one found the body?"

Booker nodded gloomily. "He's still pretty well shook up. And I don't feel so good myself. See, when I got here he was waitin' for me outside the unit, looking like he'd just dumped in his pants. I made him go back in with me. I found the kid's arm, but we didn't see any head at first. He was the one found it, where it rolled under the bed."

Booker shivered slightly and folded his arms, squinting unhappily into the bright sunshine.

"What else can you tell me, Booker?" Skip asked.

"Not much. All we know for sure is your man and Mary Lou Dobbs pulled up in her Lamborghini he was repossessing and checked into the motel. I figure she was using her wiles to convince him to back off. About one in the morning the owner heard a racket from down here somewhere, but he was too sloshed to move his ass and investigate. Besides, in this place, according to him, a little preliminary rumpus is not a bit unusual. Anyway, the disturbance didn't last long. This morning a couple leaving early passed the unit. The lights were still on, they saw the door sagging open and, inside it, pieces—well, chunks, really—of your man's body parts."

"So they alerted the motel owner?"

"Yeah."

"Where's the couple now?" Skip queried.

"They took off in a big hurry, without checking out properly and without waiting for us to get here."

"And there was no trace of Mary Lou Dobbs—or the Lamborghini."

"That's right. She was gone and so was the car."

"As I understand it, you've already called my brother."

"Yeah, about half an hour ago."

"Then you were pretty sure it was Jimmy Vasquez you had in there."

"We found his license in his wallet and your company's card in his pants pocket."

Skip glanced back through the motel's open doorway. "I figure whoever did this used an ax."

"That's what the son of a bitch used on the door. And he kept on using it when he got inside. A real freaked-out wacko." Booker shook his head. "When I walked in there this morning . . . I tell you, Skip. I never saw nothin' like it in my life."

"Which means if you pull in the bastard who did this, he'll walk."

"Sure. Since when's a raving lunatic ever been held responsible? He'll get sent to some nuthouse until the shrinks get sick of looking at him. Then out he'll come, looking for another ax."

"You've got an APB out on Mary Lou Dobbs, I suppose."

"Yep. And as soon as the chief got here, I left to check with her mother. She was no help. You listen to her, she never even had a daughter. She's been too busy watching the boob tube."

"What can you tell me about Mary Lou?"

He shrugged. "Not all that much. She's a local tramp. Blond and well-stacked. In her early twenties. Entered her profession before graduating from junior high. We figure she's into heavy stuff now, and dealing. Must be, to drive a goddamm Lamborghini."

Skip nodded.

"Looks like she didn't want to part with it."

A sheriff's patrol car pulled onto the parking lot, and right behind it came a TV news van, the call letters of an Albany ABC affiliate painted on its side. The sheriff left his red-and-white almost on the run, heading for Booker, obviously upset he hadn't been plugged into this sooner. The van braked sharply, its tires squealing on the macadam. Farther down the highway, approaching the motel, came the state trooper's BCI car, roof beacons flashing.

The circus was about to begin.

Skip started for his car.

"You leaving now?" Booker called after him.

"Comb your hair and suck in your gut," Skip told him. "You're on the six o'clock news."

Climbing into his car, Skip backed out and hit the highway, tires squealing. It was almost seven-thirty when he reached Hudson Creek. The only place open was a Sunoco gas station. The owner, working on a car up on the lift, came out of the service area wiping his hands with a red shammy cloth. Skip asked him if he could use the pay phone in his office. Nodding, the owner returned to the car on the lift. Buford answered his phone on the second ring and told him he'd just got back from seeing Jimmy's mother.

". . . and I don't never want to do anything like that again, Skip," he said. "Never again."

"You could've called her."

Bill Knott

"Yeah, sure. I could've. But would you have just called?"

"No, I guess not."

"So what the hell's going on up there?"

Skip gave Buford what he had found out so far, omitting a few of the more gruesome details, wrapping it up with the supposition that a homicidal maniac friend of Mary Lou Dobbs had taken her and the Lamborghini. He finished by telling Buford to send someone up to the Lands End Motel for the ramp truck.

"You mean you ain't coming back here?"

"Not right now."

"Where you going?"

"After Mary Lou Dobbs and that Lamborghini."

He hung up.

CHAPTER 3

FRANK SANTORINI OPENED THE BEDROOM DOOR AND ducked his head inside. Moon had just given Mary Lou a mean crack on her head, and the small room rang with the sound of it. Frank beckoned to Luigi. Luigi let go of Mary Lou's legs and followed Frank out of the room.

Frank closed the door and drew Luigi away from it. Luigi was a good-looking, olive-skinned kid from Queens with a wiry mop of Italian hair and big liquid eyes that were setting the local quiff into a prolonged heat. Carmine had sent him up here to keep him out of trouble. Fat chance.

Bill Knott

"What the fuck happened?" Frank demanded. "I just saw the bloody shirt Moon left in the bathroom sink."

"I don't know if I want to tell you, Frank."

"Luigi, don't fuck with me!"

"Honest to Christ, I couldn't stop him."

"You gonna stop twisting my dong and tell me what the hell happened?"

"Moon used an ax."

"An ax? What're you tellin' me?"

"So help me, Moon used his ax to get through the motel door—and when he got inside, he kept right on using it."

"Jesus! You mean he chopped up this here hood was with her?"

"He hacked him to fucking pieces, is what he did, Frank. He turned him into dog food. There was nothing I could do, 'cept keep out of his way and not get hit by any flying blood clots."

Frank glanced toward the bedroom. He could hear Moon's fists pounding with solid precision into Mary Lou's body and thought he could hear his grunt each time he punched. The son of a bitch was working hard. Very hard. His heart was in his work.

His real name was Howie Randall, but he answered to Moon, short for full-mooner. The mob had found him in a Georgia swamp, a hulking giant who wrestled alligators for the tourist crowd. But when he started enforcing for the mob in Atlanta, he got too enthusiastic. He tore off so many heads, the mob sent him up here to cool off. Frank found right off that he was a great bouncer, and now that word had

BODY PARTS

gotten around, there was no more trouble from the local rednecks when it came time to close the bar. He was a full mooner, all right, a wacko in the grand tradition. So far he hadn't hurt anyone who fed him regular.

But Frank was beginning to think he had just made a bad mistake sending him after Mary Lou.

"What about the muscle with her, Luigi? Didn't he use his heater?"

"He was no muscle, Frank. Just just some punk kid she latched on to. The only heater he had was between his legs. He didn't know what the hell was coming down. Whatever that cunt told you was a load of shit."

"Figures." Frank sighed. "Go on back in there. Keep that geek from tearing off her head. I don't want no blood all over the place."

Luigi slipped back into the bedroom. Frank picked up Mary Lou's pink tote bag off the sofa where he'd thrown it. He opened it and got all bent out of shape again. The shit she'd tried to pass off for the genuine stuff still filled it, the torn pieces of the Baggies she'd used gleaming brightly in the sugar. Hell, she hadn't stepped on the stuff, she'd run a goddammed steam roller over it. The only thing you'd get from this crap was diabetes.

He flung the tote bag back down onto the sofa and stood there for a moment, listened to the two of them wailing away at the stubborn little bitch and realized he needed help. He was getting that feeling he always got when things started turning to shit.

He picked up the phone and dialed a number in

Bill Knott

Albany. A sleepy, irritated voice asked who the fuck was calling this early.

"It's me," Frank said. "That you, Caesar?"

"Frank?"

"Yeah. I need you. Get up here."

"Hey, whatsamatter?"

"Just get here, will you? And don't go to my house. Come to the restaurant. You been here before, ain't you?"

"Yeah. I know the place. What's goin' down, hey, Frank?"

"Never mind that. You owe me, Caesar. I'm calling in my chits. And bring your working tools."

"You want someone whacked?" Caesar seemed to perk up nicely at the thought.

"Just get up here."

"Hey, Frank, you say it—Caesar do it."

Frank hung up, feeling a little better. Caesar was his ace in the hole, a Sicilian zip brought in to help run the pizza parlors distributing smack—until that goddamn federal task force closed down the operation. At the moment, Caesar was on the lam for whacking one of Carmine's soldiers in a private beef. It had been a bad mistake. But Frank had known the son of a bitch Caesar knocked off, and as far as Frank was concerned, the zip had done him a favor. So Frank went to Carmine and convinced him to cancel the contract he'd put out on Caesar, and now Frank was sending the zip a few bills a week while he cooled off in Albany, working for Domino's Pizza.

This particular zip was not someone Frank

BODY PARTS

wanted to get on the wrong side of. The only time Frank had seen the Sicilian lighten up was when he talked about the particulars of his profession. He favored a .22 with a suppressor attached, and liked to get close enough to his mark to place the slug just behind the ear so it would ricochet around inside the skull, tearing everything up. It worked every time, Caesar assured him.

Frank pushed open the sliding glass door and stepped out onto the deck. He crossed to the railing and watched the morning sun hit the lake, the mists on its mirrorlike surface rising like steam from a Manhattan manhole. A bit of nostalgia for Mulberry Street and Lefty Mirra's Social Club nudged him, but the moment passed and he became aware of the racket of pots and pans in the kitchen below as the cooks began their preparation for the day ahead.

He glanced at the Lamborghini parked under the deck—at what he now realized was the biggest fucking mistake in his life. Frank shook his head. When that little bitch called him last night, he'd had a shit fit and fell in it. She'd told him she'd brought professional Colombian muscle up from Miami who would take him apart if he didn't pay off the car. Like it was his fault it wasn't paid off. So he'd sent Moon and Luigi after her. The trouble was, he'd been so pissed off at the cunt's gall, he'd lit a fire under Moon. Frank shook his head. It was like he had pressed the wrong button—or pressed the right button too hard.

What he had hoped in the first place was that Mary Lou would stay in Miami. She had become too visible a plaything up here, so he'd taken her down there, got her the car and bought them both a condo right on the water. And he'd left a bundle with her, enough to pay off the car and fix up the condo. Instead, what did she do? Drove up here in that fucking car and used his money to go into business for herself. Competing with *him*, for Christ sake, with his own money!

Not only that, but he had begun to hear things about her setting up a crack factory. Crack! Up here in lovely, high-toned Lake Placid. Crack meant losers—wild-eyed crazies foaming at the mouth, spraying the neighborhood with Uzi's. It would stir up the whole damn community, drive Horse Face and the rest of her high-toned friends wild. The way it was now, he was selling a very high-quality product to a well-heeled clientele at high-class prices. He was making no waves, simply providing a service. And here was that crazy little bitch fixing to flush all that down the toilet.

He left the railing, slid back the glass door and poked his head into the living room to listen. Luigi and Moon were still in the bedroom working her over. He could hear them through the door. Christ, she was as tough as she was stupid. She'd wear them both out.

He slid the glass door back and slumped into the chaise longue.

Until his own exile to Lake Placid, Frank had been a failure—worse, he had been a dangerous liability. In an effort to make an impressive hit, he and some of Carmine's soldiers attempted to rob a garment factory. The trouble was, they hit the place at the

BODY PARTS

end of the day shift, and when the husbands came to pick up their wives, the resulting hassle raised a stink loud enough to alert half of Brooklyn. When Frank tried to hold one of the hysterical women hostage, she nearly scratched his eyes out. He got over a back fence safely, but a few of Carmine's soldiers went to the slammer, and some of them were still there. What made it so bad was that since he hadn't cleared the heist with Carmine before going in, the don thought Frank had planned to hold out on him.

The only reason he hadn't been whacked for this royal fuck-up was the don owed his old man—that, and the fact that no one wanted to spend enough money for a legitimate contract, which showed Frank just how thoroughly worthless he had become in the eyes of the family. All he had going for him now was that Carmine still revered his old man enough to send him up here to run the restaurant for the family—after warning Frank to keep his ass so far down he should maybe consider himself already dead and buried.

And that's how low he had hunkered for two long miserable years in this goddamn icebox—until he met Carlotta Calhoun, a lonely horse face of a widow with so much money it was like an albatross around her neck, her exact words. When he saw how eager she was to spread her green around, he got interested real fast and made his play. Like she put it later, his dark good looks swept her off her feet.

They got married, like in the movies, and the don came all the way up from New Jersey to give his

Bill Knott

blessing. Frank moved to Carlotta's ten-acre estate and began driving the kind of cars he always knew he should. For his last birthday she had left a midnight-black Jag sitting in the front drive, a big red ribbon wrapped around it. With the money she piled on to him, he'd long since gone into business. He had found Lake Placid almost virgin territory, able to absorb as much as he could deal. And now he was piling up the loot so fast he was sweating to find places to stash it.

The phone rang inside. He left the deck and answered it.

"Frankie?"

It was Carlotta. From the tone of her voice he could tell she was pouting.

"Hi, Carlotta."

"I just woke up and I turned over and you weren't there."

"I already told you. The cook lit out, and I'm having trouble getting another. I've been calling all over the place. It's a real bummer."

"But I need you here. Now. Beside me."

He glanced at his watch. "I'll be back up at the house before eight, honey. Just keep the bed warm."

"You know what I need, don't you?"

"Sure, honey. I know."

"A kiss where it'll do the most good."

"Take a shower. And put on that new perfume I got you. I'll be right there."

"Hurry home, lover."

She gave the phone a loud, wet kiss and hung up.

He looked at the phone in disgust and dropped it

into the cradle, then slumped down onto the sofa, hearing clearly now the sounds coming from the bedroom.

Before he and Carlotta were married, when he was finally allowed the royal privilege of getting into her pants, he'd gone down on her right off and it had blown her fucking mind. No one had ever done that to her before, she told him. What he guessed was no one would have dared. Anyway, for what she claimed was the first time in her life, she got her rocks off.

So she had no complaints on that score. If anyone had complaints, he did. Not that she didn't like it. He had never known such a genuinely horny bitch. But it was like tuning a piano. Or trying to. She'd lie on her back until he'd pushed her over the edge—which took awhile—and once it began, she could keep on coming forever, and he would end up too pooped-out to climb aboard and take his turn. At first he had expected that out of pure gratitude if nothing else Horse Face would at least give him some head. No way. He hinted around plenty, and when he finally presented himself for the favor, all scrubbed and clean, she was shocked. How could he think she would do such a thing?

Which made him wonder what she really thought of him.

Not that it mattered all that much.

Early on he'd found this crazy little nympho working for him as a waitress. What brought Mary Lou to his attention was word she was going into business for herself, turning tricks for the customers. To put a stop to that nonsense, he made her a hostess and set her to work servicing him. Best action he'd ever had. Bazongers that made him believe in the divinity. A high, tight ass, and a way of moving said, Come one, come all—and this little lady had absolutely no qualms about going down on him. Hell, she enjoyed it as much as he did.

It was a goddamn shame the little shit had crossed him like this. After all he'd done for her.

The bedroom door opened. He looked over. Moon was standing in the doorway. The big, hulking son of a bitch actually looked tired. Luigi stepped out after him and pulled the door shut, like he was anxious to hide an indiscretion. Frank could imagine what shape Mary Lou was in, but it was her own goddamn fault. From the look on their faces, he could tell she had finally spilled her guts.

Frank got to his feet. "Well, where's she got it hid?"

Luigi said, "She didn't want to tell us because she was afraid we'd hurt her old lady. She left it back in her house, stashed behind the water tank in the bathroom."

"Real original."

"Yeah."

"How much did she leave there?"

"Four keys."

"Four *keys?* That crazy little dipshit." He glanced at the closed bedroom door. "How is she?"

Luigi looked at Moon. The big man shifted his feet. "She's still breathin'."

"Tie her up good. I don't want her goin' nowhere.

And then get that Lamborghini out of sight. Dump it somewhere."

"You want us to go after them four kilos?" Luigi asked.

"What the hell do you think?" Frank demanded, exasperated. "But first dump the car—and when you get back with the stuff, call me. I'll be up at the house."

He had no intention of glancing into the bedroom to check on Mary Lou's condition, even though she had given him some real good times. All that was in the past. As far as he was concerned, she no longer existed. Besides, Horse Face was waiting. He brushed past Luigi and hurried downstairs, then cut swiftly through the empty restaurant. Outside, through the bright early morning sun, he crunched across the gravel to his Jaguar.

As soon as Luigi closed the bedroom door, Mary Lou rolled off the bed and crawled on all fours to the door leading out to the back hall. She could barely see out of one side of her face, and she had to keep her mouth open in order to breathe. She reached up for the knob, pulled the door open, slipped out into the hall, then crawled headfirst down the stairs. When she came to the first turn, she almost cried out as her bruised shoulder brushed against the wall.

At the foot of the stairs she crawled through the first door she came to and found herself out on the small loading platform. Turning back, she pushed through the double doors into the kitchen. Her shoulder came hard against a man's leg, clothed in greasy white work pants. It was painful for her to look up, but she managed it and saw Ahmed, the cook's helper, peering down at her. She glanced quickly around. The cook, Benson, was not in sight.

"Hey, there, little mother," Ahmed said, his shiny black face creasing into a brilliant grin. "Welcome to the kitchen staff." He dropped the plucked chicken he was washing. "What're you doin' down there?"

"Help me, please, Ahmed."

He bent close. "You don't look so good, little mother. Your face look like raw beef. You must've had bad people workin' you over."

"It's Moon and Luigi. If I don't get away, they'll kill me!"

"Now what you done?"

She was too tired to lie. "I was dealin'."

"Hey, you crossin' the Man? I can't help you. Lose my job."

"Ahmed, you like me. You said so."

"You offerin' this black man some white pussy?"

"Whatever you want . . . please, help me."

"You don't look so good, little mother. You sure you can still pleasure a man?"

"Try me," she gasped.

"Maybe I will. I heard tell you got a very educated mouth. Get up off that filthy floor and follow me."

She tried to push herself upright, but the pain in her right side halted her. Panting, she slumped forward, one palm sliding over the greasy floor into a pile of potato peelings. She heard footsteps pound-

BODY PARTS

ing down the back stairs. Ahmed heard them, too. He reached down with one hand, grabbed her by the back of her tank top and, lifting her as easily as if she were one of those plucked chickens he was washing, strode over to the walk-in meat cooler. He opened the door and dropped her inside. A ratty fur coat was hanging on a hook inside the door. He threw it onto her.

"Stay cool, baby," he said and closed the door.

Oh, God, it was so cold! And dark! She wrapped the coat around her, but the chill was already seeping into her bones. Through chattering teeth she murmured frantically, "Holy Mary, Mother of God, if I get out of this, I'll be a good girl. I promise. I won't do nothin' bad no more. Oh, Mother of God, please hear my prayer!"

She began to cry softly. The freezer's penetrating cold seeped into her battered body. She pulled the coat closer about her.

When Luigi saw the empty bedroom, he halted, stunned. Grunting an obscenity, Moon brushed past him and barged through the bedroom and out the other door to the back stairs. Luigi followed him down them into the restaurant. A quick lope through it, looking under tables, behind the bar, even checking both rest rooms, brought them back to the dining area. They charged through the swing doors into the kitchen.

The day cook, Benson, glanced back at them as he

slowly, carefully, lowered a huge pot onto the stove. Ahmed was farther down at the sink, washing off chickens, the hot water running steadily down over the naked birds.

Luigi halted. "Either of you seen Mary Lou?"

"Was she wearing anything?" Benson cracked, reaching for a wooden ladle.

"This is serious, goddammit," Luigi said.

"Hey, look, kid," the cook said, turning about to face them, "I'm gettin' ready for a busy day. You and Moon can stay in here and watch, if you want. But don't blame me if you've lost your playmate."

"We all had her upstairs," Moon told him anxiously. "The dumb bitch ran away. She must've come down here."

"Be my guest. Look anywhere you want. In the pots. The pans. Closets. Shelves. Under the sink. The incinerator. And if you find her, I want sloppy seconds."

"Yeah," said Ahmed, grinning over at them from the sink. "Me, too."

Luigi and Moon did a quick, cursory search of the kitchen, pushed out through the double doors onto the loading platform and jumped down onto the gravel. Splitting up, they searched opposite ends of the parking lot. When they came together at the foot of the steps leading up to the deck, Moon was so frustrated he was close to tears.

"Maybe she's still up there," Luigi suggested desperately. "Hiding in a closet or something."

Moon grunted hopefully and the two of them ran up the steps. But after a feverish search of the

BODY PARTS

closets and every other possible hiding place in the apartment, they realized Mary Lou was gone.

"Jesus Christ, Moon," Luigi said, standing on the deck and peering distractedly across the lake, as if there were a chance he might catch sight of Mary Lou in a canoe or something, paddling furiously away from them. "Frank ain't goin' to like this."

Moon nodded, his face a mask of pure frustration. "So maybe we better haul ass and get rid of that Lamborghini, then get them kilos Mary Lou stashed in her old lady's house."

They hurried back down the steps to the parking lot and came to a halt in front of the Lamborghini. Luigi stared at it, fascinated. In the slanting rays of the early morning sun, it had the clean glow of something alive, like a bird—a sea gull, maybe. Driving it the night before had almost given him an erection. All that power. He could feel it pulsing under his foot, waiting to be unleashed.

"Damn," Luigi said reverently, "it's a pure shame to get rid of this boat. You know what one of these costs?"

Moon was not thinking of the Lamborghini's price tag. He was thinking of what Frank would say if they didn't get rid of it like he said. "You think maybe we should dump it in the lake?" he suggested hopefully.

"Hell, no, you dumb shit. You know what that baby costs? I'll drive the Lamborghini. You follow me in your car."

As Luigi got into the Lamborghini, Moon loped over to his Trans Am.

Bill Knott

Not quite halfway between Hudson Creek and Lake Placid, Luigi swung the Lamborghini off the highway onto a narrow logging road, Moon keeping close on his tail. Half a mile into the pines the logging road petered out. Luigi kept going, crossed a large field of cut-over timber and kept on through the slash, the car rolling smoothly, silently, over the slick carpet of pine needles. When he came to a solid stand of uncut timber blocking his way, he got out and walked over to the edge of the clearing and up onto a small ridge he had spotted. Yep. It was just the spot he was looking for.

He returned to the car, told Moon to back his Trans Am out of his way, backed up the Lamborghini, cut right, then eased it forward down a slight slope into a hollow under the ridge. He turned off the ignition, pocketed the keys, and used his handkerchief to wipe away any fingerprints on the dash, door handle, and steering wheel. Still using the handkerchief, he swung up the gull wing door and climbed out, slammed the door shut and joined Moon on the ridge.

"Y'all going to leave it out here?" Moon asked.

"That ax still in your car, Moon?"

Moon nodded.

"Cut off as many pine branches as you can. We'll cover up this beautiful sucker. Bury it. Frankie told us to dump it. But he didn't say where or how. When the time comes, we'll come back for it. You and me. I know a man can file off the engine's ID number. Hell, when we cash this baby in, we'll be able to go into business for ourselves."

"Well, Ah don't know," Moon drawled. "Cuttin' all them branches'll take time, an' we gotta get outta here. Frank wants them kilos Mary Lou stashed, Luigi."

Luigi shrugged, surprised at Moon's good sense. "Yeah, maybe you're right. We can always come back later when we have more time."

When they reached the Trans Am, Moon said, "Hey, Luigi, you drive. I lost my way a couple of miles back."

"Sure. No sweat."

Luigi got in behind the wheel, waited for Moon to climb in beside him, turned the Trans Am around and drove back along the ridge, his mind alert to a new possibility. Hell, if this crazy hillbilly didn't know how to find his way *out* of here, didn't that mean he'd have a hell of a time finding his way back in?

Well, now. That left only him who knew where he'd stashed the boat. So maybe, when the time was ripe, he'd come back in here all by his lonesome and drive it off himself.

No sense in cutting in King Kong if he didn't have to.

Skip thanked the Sunoco dealer, got back into his car and drove down Main Street, turned onto Canal and a moment later pulled up in the driveway of Mary Lou Dobbs's house. He slammed the car door loud enough to alert the girl's mother or anyone else in the house. A tiny hairless dog with a filthy rope knotted around its neck stuck its head out from around the corner of the house. Too dispirited even to bark, at one glance from Skip it ducked back out of sight, its ratlike tail snugged tightly into its quivering anal cleft. The front door opened and a Pillsbury Woman in her late forties, wearing a faded blue print housecoat, her hair resplendent in pink curlers, stepped out onto the porch. Blinking in the bright morning sunlight, she shaded her eyes and peered down at him.

"Hello, ma'am," Skip said, smiling broadly.

While he was on the Albany force, whenever he made inquiries in a strange neighborhood, he found it helped if those he interrogated thought he was not too bright. It was amazing what people would reveal to someone they considered not quite as smart as they were.

"What do you want?" the woman asked warily, pulling her housecoat more tightly around her. "The police was just here and I already told them I don't know nothin' about that dead man."

"Why, sure you don't," Skip told her emphatically, bouncing up the sagging porch steps.

"Oh, ain't you a cop?" she said, stepping back.

"No, ma'am. I sure ain't."

Skip headed confidently for the door. Mary Lou's mother moved out of his way, and Skip kept on past her into the house and abruptly found himself standing in the living room. As the woman padded in after him and closed the door, he took off his hat and coat and handed them to her. She looked distractedly about her for a moment, then took his hat and coat into what he presumed to be a bedroom off the hallway.

Skip sat down on the living room couch.

The tiny room was claustrophobic. Its two windows were darkened by dusty drapes drawn permanently to facilitate daylight TV viewing. Cluttered shelves covered the walls, shrinking the living area appreciably. Where there was no room for shelves, the walls were covered with pictures, faded and scarcely visible in the dim light. On the wall above the TV four or five Palm Sunday palm fronds, dusty now and stiff with age, were tucked behind a familiar painting of the Lord. The TV set was on, tuned to an early morning network news show, the volume just loud enough to be annoying.

Mary Lou's mother returned to the living room and sat down in a padded rocker facing the television. With surprisingly delicate fingers she adjusted the faded housecoat about her loose expanse and glanced at the tube, then at him. He knew then that there was no way in hell she was going to turn the goddamn thing off. Pink mules clung to her swollen, lumpy feet. Her face sagged, her eyes were moist and sorrowful.

Ignoring the disaster unfolding at his elbow—a helicopter shot of a burning oil refinery—he cleared his throat and leaned forward expectantly, in this way silently prodding her to speak first. With a great effort of will, she looked away from the tube.

"I guess maybe you're waitin' for Mary Lou."

"Not exactly, Mrs. Dobbs."

"Mrs. Dobbs? Oh, no, that ain't my name. Not no more. I changed it when I divorced Mary Lou's father. I got my own name back. You can do that now. My name's Dilman. Violet Dilman."

"Your husband around, Violet?"

Startled, she glanced nervously about her. "What husband?"

"You mean you didn't marry again?" he remarked, shooting wildly in the dark. "Mary Lou said—"

"Oh, you mean Ray."

"I guess."

She sat back in her rocker, for the first time looking completely away from the tube. "Well, no, Ray ain't here. He left long ago. I'm surprised Mary Lou even remembered him. But we never tied the knot, so to speak."

Skip nodded. He had just managed to convince the woman that Mary Lou and he were more than acquaintances. How else could he have known about Ray?

"Violet, did the police tell you what happened—at the motel, I mean?"

She pulled her housecoat closer about her, as if she felt a sudden draft. "They told me they found a dead man there. They said Mary Lou went to the motel with him. I told them they made a mistake. She wasn't even there last night."

"How do you know that, Violet?"

"Because last night she came back here for her tote bag with two men, and she never said nothin' to me about no murder." She frowned, as if forcing herself to remember. "Thing is, I could see she'd been crying some. But she told me not to worry none, said she was fine and she'd be back soon's she could. Said she had an insurance policy to pick up."

"Mary Lou's a real crafty one," Skip acknowledged. "Yes, sir. No need to worry about her."

"You mean you ain't jealous—her leavin' with them two men?"

"Why should I be?"

"Ain't you that gentleman friend Mary Lou's been seeing in Lake Placid? The one who gave her that lovely new car?"

"Of course I ain't jealous. I can trust Mary Lou."

"Oh my, yes, you surely can. I didn't mean to say nothing against Mary Lou. There's some in town say she's wild, but she's always been good to her mother."

"Those two men with her, did you get a good look at them?"

She thought back and made a face. "One of them wasn't very nice at all, kept using them four-letter words. He was real big and looked mean. I could tell Mary Lou didn't like him. But the other one was a nice young Italian boy with curly hair."

"Violet, did you tell the sergeant about those two men?"

"I wouldn't tell that Henry Booker nothin'. He's always had it in for my Mary Lou. Besides, they told me not to say a word about them."

"When did Mary Lou tell you about this insurance policy, Violet?"

"She whispered it in my ear when she left."

"Have you ever seen the policy?"

"Why, no. I never even knew she had one."

"Tell you what, Violet, I'm here to pick up some of Mary Lou's things. She was in such a hurry, she didn't get to pack all she needed."

"Oh."

Violet kept trying to look back at the TV screen.

"Maybe you could pack some of her things," Skip suggested. "I'm expecting her to stop over at my place later."

Violet looked at him. "Your place?"

He winked. "Maybe we'll take a trip somewhere."

"Oh, you mean you might be goin' back to Miami?"

"We really loved it down there."

"Mary Lou, she said it was awful hot."

Like a field mouse no longer able to avoid the snake's hypnotic stare, Violet glanced back at the tube. The morning news show was over and a game show had taken its place. A giant multicolored wheel was turning slower and slower, and a woman was jumping up and down in front of it, clapping her hands. The wheel stopped and the woman threw her arms around the game-show host's neck and, still jumping up and down, thrust herself hard against him, her face tucked against his cheek. The host took his time unwinding the woman's arms from around his neck. A shot of the audience showed steep tiers of ecstatic women applauding wildly.

BODY PARTS

Violet looked back at Skip. "I'll go pack Mary Lou's things. Would you like a cup of coffee?"

"I wouldn't want to put you to any trouble."

"Oh, it's no trouble at all," she said, heaving herself out of the rocker.

Evidently she'd concluded that if she were going to get in her full day in front of the tube, she'd better pack her daughter's things and send him on his way. With a quick parting glance at the screen, she slipped from the living room and disappeared into the kitchen.

Skip waited until he heard the coffeepot rattling before he got up and checked out the bedrooms. There were two across the hall from each other. It was not difficult to tell which one was Mary Lou's. Peering in through the doorway, he saw a mess that could not have been due entirely to Mary Lou's hasty departure. Tank tops, panty hose, pumps, skirts, brassieres, lingerie, silk blouses, baby-doll nightgowns, and bikini panties were strewn over the unmade bed, the floor, the top of the dresser—over any available surface.

The bathroom, he saw, opened off her bedroom.

"Mind if I use the bathroom?" Skip called to Violet.

"Go right ahead!"

He winced. The woman was so easy.

He stepped into Mary Lou's bedroom and did a swift, expert search in the dresser drawers, under her bed and between her mattress and the box spring for that insurance policy she had mentioned. Then he entered the bathroom, closed the door and

Bill Knott

found what he was looking for almost at once. Mary Lou had jammed a paper bag down behind the water tank, precisely where ninety percent of all addicts stashed their goods.

He pulled out the bag, opened it, and whistled softly when he saw how much of an insurance policy Mary Lou had left behind. He counted four kilos at least, each one inside a plastic Baggie fastened with a neat red plastic tie. He opened one of them, poked into it with a moist finger and tasted it. The snow had been stepped on, but it was still at least eighty percent or better. He closed the Baggie, took the others out of the bag and wrapped them inside a beach towel. After flushing the toilet, he stepped out of the bathroom.

Violet was standing by the bed, packing Mary Lou's overnight bag. She glanced up. Without comment Skip reached past her and placed the folded towel into it. Violet snugged it against the side and continued packing, adding two more blouses and some black silken undergarments before forcing the blue suitcase shut.

Thanking her, Skip took it and walked back into the living room. A cup of coffee waited for him on a TV tray in front of the couch. He placed the suitcase on the floor beside him and sat down.

His was a cruel deception, he realized, and he got no pleasure taking advantage of Violet in this fashion; but he was comforted by the certainty that no matter what calamity befell her, in the end she would dry her tears and return to her picture tube

BODY PARTS

and find all the comfort she needed in its soothing banalities.

A car drove into the yard.

Violet was on her way back into the living room when she heard the car pull up. She hurried to the window and, nudging a drape aside, peered out.

"Oh, here they are!" she said. "They've come back!"

Beside her in a moment, Skip saw two men getting out of a black Trans Am that had just pulled in alongside his Mazda.

"Mary Lou's not with them," Violet said. "I wonder where she is?"

That's what Skip was wondering, but he had no problem figuring out why these two had returned.

They were after Mary Lou's insurance policy.

CHAPTER 4

Skip pulled Violet away from the window.

"Violet, do you have a friend nearby?"

She glanced back at the window, confused. "What's that?"

"Do you have a neighbor you can visit—share a cup of coffee with while you catch up on the local gossip."

"Oh! You mean Arabelle."

"How far is she?"

"Only two houses up."

"Can you go by a back way?"

"You mean along the river?"

Bill Knott

"I think you should visit her now."

"Now?"

"Yes."

She looked distractedly about her, then glanced down at her housecoat. "I'll have to change."

"No, you won't. Go as you are."

Violet was bewildered. "But I don't know if Arabelle's home!"

Skip leaned close to her. "If Arabelle's not there," he said urgently, "go inside and wait for her."

"Oh, I couldn't do that."

"Violet, listen to me. You're in danger."

"Me?"

She glanced back at the tube. The game-show host was clapping his hands as he stepped to one side. The Wheel of Fortune or whatever the hell it was began to whirl, the colors blurring. Skip stepped over to the set and turned it off.

"Violet, go see Arabelle."

He took her by the shoulders and spun her around, then slapped her plump fanny. With a startled cry she lurched into the kitchen, her slippers smacking loudly on the linoleum. Skip followed after her, and as she pushed through the screen door, he caught it and closed it silently behind her, then watched her cut behind a lilac bush. A second later he saw her pink curlers bobbing along a path toward a small white-frame house.

Violet had dumped his hat and coat on her bed. Shrugging into his coat, he clapped on his hat and ducked back into the living room to peer out through a narrow slit in the window drape's worn fabric.

BODY PARTS

The big one—he looked like a TV wrestler whose head had slammed a corner post too many times—was standing alongside the Mazda, staring intently at the Mohawk Indian peering out at him from the decal. The one Violet had described as a nice Italian boy was in the Mazda's front seat, completing a search of the glove compartment. As Skip watched, the dago pushed himself out of the car and slammed the door. A sharp dresser, he was wearing a gleaming gray suit and tie, complete with vest, that had to have set him back a thousand clams, at least. As he started for the front porch, he waved the big fellow around to cover the back of the house.

Skip grabbed Mary Lou's suitcase and hustled back out through the kitchen door, pausing long enough to keep the screen door from slamming, then cut the other way around the house to avoid the big fellow. With the dog cowering in terror just behind him, Skip peered around the corner of the porch and waited for the Italian kid to enter the house. He watched him knock once, sharply, try the door, then push inside.

Skip darted across the yard to his car, dumped Mary Lou's blue overnight bag into his backseat, and slipped in behind the wheel. Glancing back at the house, he saw the dago standing in the doorway. Skip slammed the door, gunned the car to life and backed out, memorizing the Trans Am's license number as he did so.

Jouncing into the street, he cut the wheel sharply and floored the accelerator. At the end of the dirt lane he hung a right onto a gravel road and followed it until he reached the alley leading onto the town's main drag. He braked at the mouth of the alley for the traffic flow, then glanced into his rearview mirror and saw the Trans Am slew wildly into the alley behind him.

He booted the Mazda out in front of an eighteen-wheeler. As the semi farted and bleated in indignation, Skip cut down Hudson Creek's main street and headed out of town. Behind him the Trans Am swung out across the double line to get around the semi, then roared up fast to overtake him. It was swinging out again to pull alongside when the Lands End Motel came in sight.

Two blue-and-golds remained on the scene, their flashing roof beacons very much in evidence. The driver of the Trans Am saw the roof beacons, hit his brakes and dropped back swiftly. Watching the Trans Am in his rearview mirror, Skip spun his wheel and jounced onto the motel parking lot. Behind him the Trans Am made a U-turn and, tires smoking, sped back to Hudson Creek. Booker, talking to a couple of troopers near one of the patrol cars, glanced over at Skip's approaching Mazda with a frown, then started toward him.

Skip waved, spun the wheel and regained the highway.

The Trans Am was not yet out of sight. He followed it through Hudson Creek, then hung back to allow two shield cars to fill the space between. About half an hour later, as they neared Lake Placid, Skip lapped the two cars. But as he swung back over the double line, a Winnebago as big as a Greyhound

BODY PARTS

bus eased cautiously out of a gas station in front of him and planted its big ass in his face. Twice on the narrow, twisting two-lane highway he tried to pass the oversized sonofabitch, but each time was forced to cut back behind it. Keeping well within the speed limit, the R.V. lumbered along in front of him until they reached Lake Placid, by which time Skip and the Winnebago had become part of a solid conga line of traffic.

And the Trans Am was no longer in sight.

Skip turned into Lake Placid's business district and followed a busy, congested street paralleling Mirror Lake. He stayed on it until he had circled the lake and was back in the business district. He saw no sign of the black Trans Am. Driving more slowly, he cut down side streets, glided through parking lots, parked in driveways, then circled the lake another time, naggingly aware that the Trans Am might not have entered Lake Placid at all and could still be heading north.

But he didn't really think so. Even a casual glance had told him those two goons were not your typical north country natives, especially considering how that young dago was dressed. Lake Placid was a resort for the six-figure crowd that could afford a hideaway this far north of Lake George. It was the only town around where you'd find anyone wearing threads that overpriced.

Skip pulled into the Thunderbird Motor Inn, took Mary Lou's blue suitcase from the car, and registered. In his room on the third floor, he dropped the suitcase on the bed and walked over to the window to look down at the traffic inching past the motel. He watched it hopefully for a while, then gave up and left the window to call Buford.

"Skip? Where the hell are you?"

Skip sat down on the bed. "Lake Placid."

"You get the Lamborghini?"

"Not yet. Look, Buford, I think maybe you better put Wally in charge down there. Looks like I might be up here for a while."

"You got any kind of a line on the Lamborghini?"

"Not yet."

"Skip, I just got through talking to the dealer. This Lamborghini ain't that new one Chrysler's peddling, it's a Countach. Close to two hundred gee's. Someone put a gun to the dealer's head so he'd let it go with only a few bills up front. The poor sonofabitch'll lose his shirt *and* his agency if we don't get this car back for him."

"Who was it put the gun to his head?"

"A mob figure. He won't tell me who. Afraid of getting himself blown away if he squawks too loud. The thing is, he had figured taking it back from the girl would be no sweat."

"He figured wrong. He should've told us all this before."

"Skip, do you know what our cut will be if we recover that boat?"

"It better be enough. What I want from you now is to patch me through to Terry, have her call me here."

"This mean you're on to something?"

"Just do this for me, will you, Buford?"

Buford sighed. "What's your number?"

Skip read off the phone number to Buford. "If you can't get through to her, call me back."

He hung up, dropped his head back onto the pillow, closed his eyes, and within ten minutes Terry was on the line.

"What's this all about, Skip?"

"I have a license number I want you to trace."

"Skip, you know I can't do that."

"No, I don't. Here's the number."

He gave her the Trans Am's license plate number, waited, then repeated it.

"All right. I got it. How long will you be at this number?"

"Long as it takes. I'm at the Thunderbird in Lake Placid."

"Skip, I'm sorry about this morning."

"That's all right, Terry."

"I heard about . . . what happened to that boy. How awful. I know how badly you must feel."

"Thanks, Terry."

Skip hung up and lay back, his arms folded under his head. He did not have long to wait. Less than ten minutes later the phone rang. He reached over and lifted the receiver. Crisply, Terry gave him the information he had requested. The car's owner was Howard Randall. His address was Box 134, Barrel Hill Road, Carlton, New York.

"Where's Carlton?" Skip asked, writing it down.

"A few miles north of Lake Placid."

"Anything on this Howard Randall?"

"Zilch."

"Okay. Thanks, Terry."

"Skip, how does this man figure in the Jimmy Vasquez killing?"

"I'm not sure, Terry. What I'm after now is the Lamborghini."

"Skip, if you've got something solid on this terrible business, I think you should contact Captain Carmody. He's working out of Troop B at Ray Brook. That's not far from Lake Placid."

"I don't think so, Terry."

"In heaven's name, Skip, why not?"

"I already met Captain Carmody."

"Skip, he's very highly regarded!"

"That so?"

"Larry is *very* intelligent. He has a degree in criminology and a master's in sociology. Right now he's working on his doctorate."

Skip lay back on the bed and gazed up at the ceiling. He said nothing.

"Are you there, Skip?"

"Sure. Right here."

"Skip, Larry's score on the academy's entrance exam was the highest of any recruit. He was first in rank when he graduated, and everyone sees him as a rising star in the troopers. He's the new breed, Skip, what the commissioner is looking for—and I can see why. He's not some hulking hyperthyroid with muscles for brains. And I'm sure if you contacted Larry with anything solid, he would be very grateful."

"You finished?"

"Yes," she said, her voice trailing off warily. "I'm finished."

"Terry, I just told you. I'm after the Lamborghini, that's all."

"Why do I have the feeling you're not leveling with me, Skip?"

"Thanks for tracing that license number for me, Terry."

He hung up then, before he could say something that would make them both sorry. He left the motel and crossed the street, descending concrete steps to a small lakeside sandwich shop he'd spotted from his window.

On a deck that stuck out over the water, he sat down at a white metal umbrella table and ordered a Coors and a BLT on toast. As he crunched into the sandwich and sipped his Coors, he watched the paddle boaters and the small sailboats on Mirror Lake, their multicolored sails as bright as a child's new toy.

Larry, was it? Jesus.

He finished the BLT and ordered another Coors. This lake, unlike the larger Lake Placid nearby, was kept quiet for the tourists; no power boats were allowed, especially those new motorized surfboards. In addition to those in the sailboats, a few tanned young men were perched on bright, laminated windsurfing boards. There was not enough wind to fill their sails, and they weren't really getting anywhere, but that didn't seem to bother them any.

Sixteen years before, when he and Louise had come up here on their honeymoon, everything had been much quieter, fewer cars, fewer people, and more room. The cabin they'd taken at the Mirror

Bill Knott

Lake Lodge had put him back only sixty dollars a night at the time, but even then it was an unheard of extravagance, especially on a patrolman's salary.

He had often tried to think back on that week with pleasure, to extract from it some meager straw of satisfaction, but the truth of it was that it had been a disaster, starting from the moment he had taken Louise for a canoe ride and she had told him that she intended to continue working at the real estate agency so they could put money aside for a larger house in a better neighborhood. Unwilling to believe he was hearing right, he insisted that all he wanted was a home with her in it—he didn't care about the size of the house or the neighborhood—that now, while they were young, was the time to start a family—and with the canoe gliding across the lake's slick surface, he had leaned close to her and told her that all he really needed to make him perfectly happy were two things.

"Just two things?" A tiny frown appeared on her face, and she brushed back a lock of her honey-blond hair. "Is that all?"

He nodded. "You heard me."

"I can't stand the suspense."

"A clean house, and you at home when our kids return from school."

Her expression changed, like a small cloud passing before the sun. She leaned back for a moment, her eyes studying him carefully to see if perhaps he wasn't making fun of her.

"You serious, Skip?"

"Of course."

"You said children. How many? Have you got that figured out, too?"

"As many as we can have," he said without hesitation. "A family is what I want. Isn't that what you want? I've never had a family—or a home. You know that."

"Yes, I know that. And neither have I, now that you mention it."

"Exactly." He lifted the oar out of the water and leaned back in the canoe. He had caught something in her eyes he had never seen before, and it frightened him. He knew at once that he had blundered terribly. "Don't you see?" he went on lamely. "Now we can have what both of us missed. We can have our own family and make our own home—together."

"As long as it's clean."

"Come on, Louise. You know what I mean. I hate slobs. I can't live in a place that's dirty and cluttered."

"Yes." Her lips compressed into a severe line. "I know."

"Hey, I didn't mean anything by that. All I'm sayin' is, I'll take care of the bills, you take care of the house."

"And your children."

"Our children."

She looked shoreward then at the palatial homes and mansions gleaming in the afternoon sun, their lawns sloping down to the lake shore, a hint of rebellion in her suddenly cold, blue eyes.

From that moment on Louise had withdrawn into herself, so that whenever he reached out for her again, he felt her inner self remaining aloof, indifferent. For him, at least, the real Louise wasn't there anymore.

"Will that be all?"

The waitress was bending over the table as she placed his second glass of Coors down before him. He nodded to her and reached for the frosted glass gratefully. He sipped the ice cold brew, vaguely disappointed with himself for dwelling so much on the past. Was there anything more futile, he wondered, than regret? He leaned back and let the sun warm him as he gazed across the lake's sparkling blue expanse.

And found himself suddenly alert. He sat up and peered intently at a building on the other side of the lake. Or rather at the Trans Am parked in the lot behind it. Through a screen of pines lining the parking lot, he could barely make out a large neon sign.

He called the waitress over.

"Do you know this town very well?" he asked her.

She frowned, on her guard instantly. "I guess so," she said cautiously.

An errant lock of auburn hair coiled against her tanned neck just under her ear. She was not beautiful, not even very pretty, but the fresh bloom of youth made her as lovely as the sunlit day itself. He smiled quickly to allay her suspicions.

"I just wanted to make sure you could help me," he explained. "I need directions from someone who's familiar with Lake Placid."

She relaxed and returned his smile. "Oh. Well, I

should be familiar with it. I've lived here all my life."

He glanced across the lake. "I'm wondering about that building over there on the far shore. There's a neon sign in front of it. Do you know the place?"

She peered across the lake at the building, then looked back at him. "That's Violi's Italian Restaurant."

"Good place to eat, is it? Real Italian food?"

She wrinkled her nose. "Used to be. We don't go there anymore."

"We?"

"My boyfriend and I."

"What happened? A new cook?"

She shrugged. "All I know is a different crowd goes there since this new guy from the city came up to take over."

"A new owner?"

"A manager, maybe. He didn't change the sign."

"What's his name?"

She looked at him sharply, and he could see the wheels beginning to turn. Maybe he was a narc.

He smiled again. "I just thought I might know him."

"His name's Frank Santorini."

"Nope, that's not the guy."

Skip took another sip of the Coors.

"They got a bouncer who's really something," the girl volunteered. "He's mean. And big. A real Hulk. I think he's on those steroids or something. That's why Tim and I stay away from the place."

Bill Knott

"Doesn't sound like your friendly family restaurant."

"Not anymore," she said.

"I can see how you feel. But then, I'm not a family. Just someone driving through, looking for good Italian food."

"Well, you might like it there, then."

"How do you get there from here? I mean, when I drove around the lake before I didn't see any sign of it."

"Take Greentree Road. That's the first right past the golf course. Keep on through the trees. It leads right down to the shore. You can't miss the restaurant."

"Thanks."

She left his table to wait on another customer. He finished the Coors, dropped a few bills on the table, and headed back across the street to the Thunderbird's parking lot.

CHAPTER 5

ALFRED BROWN WAS THE NAME AHMED'S MOTHER HAD given him when she dropped him twenty-eight years ago in Detroit. Now she was the only one he would let call him Alfred. Being a Black Muslim didn't mean he was one of those asshole blacks struttin' around in bedsheets calling on Allah to burn all the white devils; but he knew that him being a Muslim and one of the followers of that fine black orator Louis Farrakhan irritated the shit out of most white folks.

After Moon and Luigi roared off in the Trans Am, Ahmed sauntered out into the empty restaurant on what could have been a trip to the john, and returned to tell Benson he'd seen some zonked-out teenagers messing with his new red Fiero. Benson almost dropped the basket of fries he was preparing to lower into the grease pit.

As Benson rushed out to rescue his Fiero, Ahmed entered the freezer, picked up the little mother and flung her over his shoulder. Pushing through the rear kitchen door onto the loading platform, he jumped down onto the gravel and dumped Mary Lou into the back of his green '76 Ford Econoline van, ratty fur coat and all. Without uttering a sound, she landed on the mattress he always kept in there just in case. He swung shut the van's rear doors and locked them.

After glancing around to make sure no one had seen him, he returned to the kitchen and was busy trimming a stack of sirloins when a much relieved Benson came puffing back into the kitchen.

"You get 'em, boss?"

"Naw, they're gone," he said, mopping his face. "I checked out the Fiero. Nothin's missin'."

"I rapped on the window. Maybe that scared 'em off."

"Thanks, Ahmed," the cook said, humbly grateful as he lowered the frozen precut french fries into the grease basket, then walked back to the huge soup pot simmering on the stove.

Ahmed stepped away from the counter and wiped his hands off on his apron, lifted it over his head and hung it on a hook near the freezer door. Then he strolled closer to Benson, peering over the cook's shoulder as Benson stirred the macaroni and beef soup, his specialty.

Ahmed knew this drove Benson wild, anyone standing so close behind him while he worked. But mindful that Ahmed had just chased those teenage degenerates away from his Fiero, Benson said nothing and lifted the wooden spoon to his lips to test the soup. When he put the spoon down and reached over to a shelf for more seasoning, Ahmed kept right behind him, moving up on tiptoe so he could see over the man's shoulder as he selected the spices.

Benson could stand it no longer. He spun around to face Ahmed.

"Goddammit, Ahmed! Ain't you got nothin' to do but watch me?"

"I didn't want to disturb you, boss."

"Well, what the fuck do you think you been doin'?"

Ahmed shrugged in his best Stepin Fetchit manner.

"All right. All right. Jesus Christ! What do you want?"

"I got to split."

"You what?"

"I feel like shit."

"Since when?"

"Since I started washing them chickens. I been coughing a lot, too, an' my eyeballs're gettin' yellow. Maybe I got that hepatitis."

"Jesus, Ahmed! Don't *say* that!"

"Or maybe it's only a little of that there salmonella."

Bill Knott

Benson pulled back away from Ahmed, peering at him intently. "You're conning me, you bastard."

"You want I should start hackin' into that soup pot?"

"All right. All right. Go on, get the fuck out of here!"

"Hey, be cool, man. You don't need to sweat it. Parker and Raz'll be in soon."

"Shit, Ahmed, you know how much I can count on them two."

"Well, don't worry. I'm figurin' this here malaria I got'll be gone before the dinner rush."

"That's what you figure, huh?"

"Sure, boss."

"Get back here by three at the latest, you bastard."

"Yassa, boss."

"And cut out that crap."

Ahmed clapped on his tan golf cap and pushed through the doors to the loading ramp. He jumped down, reached the van, and ducked in behind the wheel, his black face alight with deviltry. On the way out of the parking lot he was careful not to spin his tires in the gravel. He didn't want to attract attention, seeing as how he was driving off with the man's private cooze.

He made a circuit of the lake, and just before reaching the business district, pulled up in front of a block of red brick apartment buildings across from the children's park along the lake shore. He climbed from the van and looked casually around before opening the van's rear doors and ducking inside.

BODY PARTS

Mary Lou was huddled under the fur coat. When he flung it off her, she began to shiver violently. He pushed open one of the van's doors a crack and saw a teenager with bright red lipstick, wearing red pedal pushers and a yellow tank top, pushing a stroller past. They had long since known each other carnally, so he waited until she disappeared down the street, then gathered up Mary Lou in his arms, butted his way out of the van and ran lightly up the stone steps into one of the buildings, and kept on up to his apartment on the third floor. Unlocking the door, he entered and dumped Mary Lou on his bed.

Panting slightly, he gazed down at her. She groaned, turned on her side and drew her knees up under her chin. He leaned over and rested the back of his hand against her cheek. It was still cold to the touch. He pulled a comforter off a closet shelf and covered her with it.

He decided he needed a drink. In the kitchen he opened up the refrigerator and took out an already opened can of tomato juice. He emptied the can into a glass tumbler he found in the sink and filled the rest of the glass with vodka. Stirring the drink with an encrusted soup spoon, he walked into his small living room and kicked off his shoes, sat back in his battered recliner and used his space command to turn on the TV. Soaps. Game shows. Talk shows. He punched off the TV, finished his drink and went across the hall to see how the little mother was getting along.

She was still on her side, the comforter pulled snugly over her shoulder, hiding her face. He sat down on the bed, pulled back the corner of the comforter and found himself looking with some amazement at all the bruises.

She opened her eyes and turned her head slightly to look at him. "Ahmed?"

"Now who the fuck you think it is?"

"I'm cold."

"So what you want me to do, make some hot soup?"

He was being sarcastic, but she didn't dig.

"Oh, thank you, Ahmed. Would you?"

"I ain't got no soup in the house."

"Anything warm, Ahmed, please."

She shuddered and pulled the comforter back up around her shoulders.

He returned to the kitchen, wondering why he was feeling like he had just been taken, shoved aside all the crap covering the counter and opened the cabinet over it. Two cans of Campbell's tomato soup sat alongside a can of beans and a can of corn. He remembered all at once the black quiff who'd left it there, coming in one night with two full paper sacks containing a quart of milk, a loaf of bread, English muffins and a dozen eggs, the soup and the beans and corn, so that right away he'd known what it felt like to have someone move in on him. He got rid of her the next day, but he kept the goods.

He used a church key to open the Campbell's soup, poured it into a saucepan he found in the oven, then remembered to add water. He heated the soup, seasoned it with salt, and let it simmer awhile, then dug a soup spoon out of the clutter in the sink and brought it to her in the saucepan, warning her to watch out, it was hot. She sat up slowly, painfully, easing herself back against the headboard. She winced slightly as she reached out for the spoon and saucepan. He sat down in the white wicker chair he'd glommed from a porch down the street and watched her as she carefully sipped each steaming spoonful.

After a moment she looked over at him and smiled. "This is delicious, Ahmed."

"Glad you like it."

"It's warming me right up." She frowned slightly. "But I'm still so sore."

"You oughta be. They worked you over pretty good. Them two white devils take real pride in their work."

She continued to sip the soup. Ahmed leaned back and found himself looking more closely at her battered face. The cold in the cooler must have held the swelling back some. Now that she was warming up, not only were her cheekbones swelling, but her nose and the skin covering her brow ridges seemed to be pushing out even as he watched.

She glanced up from the saucepan and caught the look in his eyes. "I must look awful."

"You tell them what they want to know?"

"I had to. I tried not to, but I couldn't stand it no more."

She went back to the soup. It was cooler now, and she was able to get spoonfuls past her swollen lips without sipping. It was pathetic how grateful she seemed to be for this one lousy can of Campbell's tomato soup.

"You goin' to tell Ahmed what this is all about?"

"I was dealin'," she told him miserably, "and brought up some really good stuff from Miami."

"How much?"

"Four keys."

Jesus. He'd sure as hell been selling this honky tail short. He did some rapid calculations. Four kilos made it close to one hundred and forty ounces. Stepped on down to street level, a man could get maybe a hundred or a hundred and twenty-five a gram. At twenty-eight grams to the ounce, this little mother here could have come away with close to half a million clams.

"Now how'd a dumb hooker like you get enough stash to buy all that nose candy? You good, I hear. But no workin' girl's that good."

"It was Frank."

"The man himself?"

She nodded, again wincing at the movement. "He gave me the money to make a payment on my Lamborghini and on the condo."

"A condo?"

"Yeah. He bought it as an investment. He had to find something to do with the money he's been making up here dealing. And I was supposed to stay down there, keep the condo up for him so he'd have a nice place when he flew down. And he wanted me to get a good suntan. I told him if he bought me that big white sport car, I would."

"You reneged on the deal."

"You know how hot it gets down there in the summer? And who do I know in Miami? Besides . . ." She shrugged.

"Besides what?"

"Everyone's so *old* down there. Its creepy. And if they ain't too old, they don't speak English, only Spanish. It's like a foreign country."

"Sounds like the Twilight Zone."

She brightened. "Yeah. That's it."

"What you're sayin' is you used the money Frank gave you to pay off the Lamborghini and the condo to buy them four kilos."

"Well, not all of the money. I just gave the fellow some of what I promised, then split. . . ." She smiled wanly. "He . . . was too tired to keep an eye on me."

"What you mean is you near fucked the poor son of a bitch to death, and when he passed out, you took the nose candy."

"He was a heavy user. It was almost too easy."

"But now Frank's got all that sugar you bought, and pretty soon he'll be dealing it himself."

"I guess so."

"Maybe he'll thank you when he cools down."

"I don't think so," she said unhappily, handing the empty saucepan and spoon back to him. As he took it from her, she reached up and felt the left side of her jaw, then let her fingers move up to her swollen eyebrow. She winced when she touched it.

Watching her, he said, "You should've told 'em what they wanted right off."

"Maybe, but I didn't want them to hurt Ma none."

Bill Knott

"What's your old lady got to do with this?"

"Oh, that's where I hid the cocaine. At her place."

He took the saucepan back into the kitchen, ran some water into it and left it in the sink. When he returned to the bedroom, Mary Lou was carefully easing herself down onto her back. She was probably stiffening up some.

He sat down on the edge of the bed, careful not to jounce it.

"How you feelin'?"

"Awful. I can hardly move my left arm—and whenever I move, my back hurts."

"So don't move."

She smiled at him. "I'm sure grateful to you, Ahmed. I don't know what would've happened to me if you hadn't hid me like you done."

"I didn't do so much," he told her. "Hell, I damn near froze you to death. You feelin' any warmer now?"

She nodded slightly, but her heart wasn't in it. And no reason why it should be. Damned if she wasn't looking worse every minute as the purple blotches on her cheeks and chin grew darker and the swelling around her eyes increased. He didn't much want to think of what the rest of her soft white body must look like.

She turned her head slightly to glance through the open door into the other bedroom, the one he used for a studio. From where he sat, he could see a corner of the canvas he was working on—a mountain scene, the same one he had been sweating over for a week now.

"What's that smell?" She wrinkled her nose.

"Turpentine—and some linseed oil."

"What's them for?"

"I use them. When I paint."

"Oh, you're an artist, Ahmed?"

"An artist? Hell no. I ain't reached that point yet, and I probably never will. What I do is, I paint pictures, that's all."

"Gee, that's so creative. I always wanted to do that."

"Yeah?"

"Sure. But everyone said I couldn't draw a straight line." She winced slightly and moved her body some to get into a more comfortable position.

"Drawing a straight line's got nothing to do with it."

"Well, I couldn't do it anyway."

She laid her head down on the pillow and closed her eyes.

He glanced in at the easel and the half-finished painting sitting on it. The trouble was, bein' an artist wasn't what a black man should be up to in this crazy country. A black man had to be musical, sing or tap dance, or he had to be a football, baseball, or basketball player, so he could get to do them crazy commercials for Budweiser. Whoever heard of a black landscape painter?

It was those dinks at the Ohio Correctional who conned him into this crazy dodge. They called it "self-expression" and turned themselves inside out to convince him he could make a living on the outside as an artist. He had a "precious gift," they kept

Bill Knott

tellin' him. So here he was in upstate New York, going to a crummy, two-year college art school, a kitchen commando on the side, broke most of the time—when he could be back in Detroit, supplying new BMWs and Lincolns to all the thriving body shops and cuttin' plants south of the city.

He looked back at Mary Lou. "I got to go now."

Her eyes widened in alarm. "Now?"

"You'll be cool here," Ahmed assured her. "I got to get back to the Man's kitchen."

"But you can't go now."

"Why not?"

"I got to thank you—for what you done for me."

"Forget it."

Ignoring him, she pushed aside the covers and pulled herself doggedly across the bed toward him.

"Let down your pants."

"I'm telling you, little mother, you don't have to."

"You helped me. And I promised."

He unbuckled his belt. Her nimble fingers did the rest. He lay back on the bed and stared up at the ceiling. This was what he got for sticking his neck out.

CHAPTER 6

CARLOTTA SAT UP IN THE BED AND LIFTED THE PHONE off its cradle, listened a moment, then handed it to Frank.

"Yeah?" he barked.

"It's me. Luigi. I'm back here at the restaurant."

"Did you get it?"

"No."

"What the hell you mean, no?"

"Maybe you better come down here, Frank."

Scowling, he handed the phone back to Carlotta and got out of bed. She hung up and turned to him, pouting.

Bill Knott

"You don't have to go right now, do you?"

"Ain't you had enough?"

She moved her limbs sensuously under the silk bedsheet, then drew it up off her legs so he could get a clear shot at what she was offering him. Her smile was supposed to be seductive.

"I guess I'm just insatiable," she told him.

"Yeah. Well look, honey, I got trouble down at the restaurant."

"That cook?"

"You got it."

"He can wait. Come here, lover. I'm just getting warmed up."

Frank turned his back on her and padded naked into the shower. When he came out a few minutes later, Carlotta was sitting up in bed, still pouting.

"I don't want you to go, Frank."

"That's too fucking bad, sweetheart. I got a restaurant to run, remember?"

"I been meaning to tell you. I want you to close that place. We don't need it, and besides, it's keeping you from me."

"We'll talk about it later," he told her, pulling on his pants.

"No, we'll talk about it now."

Ignoring her, he continued to dress. He'd heard all this before. He hadn't listened then and he wasn't going to listen now.

"I'll be back for supper," he told her.

"Frank! You always say we'll talk about it later, and we never do. This time I'm serious. I mean it. I want you to sell that damn wop restaurant. If you don't, I will."

"No you won't, Carlotta. First off, it ain't yours to sell. And if you don't shut up about it, I just might move into the apartment down there."

"Frank, you wouldn't!"

He laughed at her. "Sure I would."

He started to walk from the bedroom. Carlotta flounced out of the bed and rushed after him—an ungainly white fury, her pendulous breasts flapping. His first thought was how god-awful she looked. Must've gained ten pounds this past summer.

He made a half-hearted effort to duck aside as she flew at him, but when she managed to catch him on the cheek with her open palm, the sharp sting of the blow wiped the contemptuous smile off his face and filled him with a cold fury. He planted both feet solidly and buried his clenched fist deep into her flaccid belly. An explosive gasp burst from her. She doubled over. He grabbed a handful of her hair and, lifting her head, clipped her on the side of her lantern jaw with a solid right cross. He let her go and watched her crumple to the floor. Her big-boned body flowed over the rug like a batch of bread dough.

She looked up at him in horror, her face twisted grotesquely. Tears streamed down her face.

"You struck me!"

"You're goddamn right. And that was just for openers. Next time you come at me like that, I'll kick the shit out of you."

"Animal! You're an animal—a wife batterer!"

"That's right," he told her. "And don't you forget it."

He left her on the floor and hurried out of the house, down the wide steps to his Jaguar, and got in. Slamming the door, he glanced back at the broad porch and white pillars, the spacious brick and frame house set amidst grounds smoother and greener than any golf course. He was aware that in slugging old Horse Face he'd crossed a line. Maybe now she'd pull the plug on him.

Well, let her try.

Frank couldn't believe what Luigi had just told him. He jabbed a finger at Luigi.

"Let me get this straight, you fucking little dago. You let this repo man take that stash away from you —and then you *lose* him!"

Luigi nodded unhappily. Beside him the wacko was shifting his feet nervously, like he was in grammar school waiting for the switch to land.

"I ought to break both your necks!" Frank told them.

"Frank," Luigi said, "We can get this hotshot. No sweat. I took his business card out of his glove compartment."

"You crazy asshole! What do I do with that? You want me to call him up and ask him to please return the stash for a slight reward? Besides, he's a fucking civilian. He's probably already turned the stuff in."

"I don't think so, Frank."

"Didn't you say he drove into the motel, where the troopers were waiting for him?"

"What I said was we saw him drive into the motel, so we turned around and drove back here. But that ain't all there was to it."

"You gonna start makin' sense, or what?"

"Frank, I thought for sure this fellow'd have the cops on our tail, so I kept an eye out. But you know what? He never did stop at that motel. He just turned around and took after *us.*"

"He what?"

"Yeah, Frank," said Moon eagerly. "I seen him, too."

"We let him follow us," said Luigi. "I figured we could pull a switch on the bastard, but . . . we lost him in the traffic."

Frank took a deep breath and told himself to back off so he could take stock. There was no percentage in dumping on Luigi, and Moon was too fucking dumb. Might as well get pissed off at a fire hydrant. The question right now was why this repo man had tailed Luigi instead of delivering Mary Lou's stash to the cops. But maybe that wasn't so hard to figure. Could be this repo man wanted to deal. Maybe he was sick of bustin' his ass hustling deadbeats and saw a chance now to make a killing. He wouldn't be the first civilian to think he could cut himself in on a mob deal.

"What I can't figure," Luigi said, "is how that repo man knew where Mary Lou hid the stuff."

"She must've told him. So she could keep the Lamborghini." Frank looked sharply at Luigi. "You get rid of that boat like I said?"

"Yeah, we got rid of it okay."

"Where'd you leave it?"

"We lost it in the fucking wilderness. No one'll ever find it, Frank. They got plane wrecks in these mountains they ain't found yet."

"Where's Mary Lou?"

Luigi looked unhappily at Moon, then back at Frank. "We . . . lost her, Frank."

"You *what?*"

"She's gone, Frank," Luigi said, shrugging helplessly. "We can't figure it. When we went back into the bedroom to get her, she wasn't there."

"Wasn't there? Where the hell *was* she?"

"Beats the shit out of me, Frank."

Frank ran a hand through his hair. These two geeks were dropping him into deep shit. He felt himself losing control all over again, but forced himself to simmer down. He looked at the wacko.

"You losin' your touch, Moon? How come she could still move after you got through with her?"

Moon shifted his feet. He looked close to tears. "Jesus, Frank. Ah can't hardly believe it myself. Ah beat the holy shit out of her. Ah surely did."

Frank glanced back at Luigi. "She was in the bedroom. How'd she get out of it?"

"She crawled down the back stairs."

"To the restaurant?"

"Yeah."

"You know that for a fact, do you?"

"We saw her blood on the stairs."

"So where could she've gone from there? Did you look in the restaurant?"

"Of course, Frank."

"The kitchen?"

"Yeah, the kitchen, too."

"And we looked up here afterward," said Moon. "She wasn't nowhere."

"So what you're tellin' me is that silly little bitch just flapped her wings and flew away."

"Aw, c'mon, Frank," said Luigi.

"Well, don't you get it, you stupid wop? If Moon beat her up like he says he did, and she ain't here now, someone must've helped the bitch get out of here."

"Oh, shit," Luigi said, looking quickly over at Moon.

"Now, think. Who was downstairs when she crawled out of the bedroom?"

"No one, Frank," Luigi insisted. "It was empty down there. No one in the restaurant. No one in the lounge. We looked behind the bar and under every table. I swear. We even looked in the powder room and the john. Everywhere."

"That leaves the kitchen."

"I told you. We looked there, too."

"Who was in there?"

"The cook, Benson, and his helper."

"That nigger?"

"Yeah. Ahmed."

"And they saw nothing?"

"That's what they said, Frank."

"And of course you believed them."

Luigi's face went white.

"Son of a bitch," muttered the wacko.

"So let's get down there," Frank said, brushing past them.

With Frank in the lead, the three hurried down the stairs to the restaurant. Pushing into the kitchen, they saw Benson busy at the stove, so intent on a large pot of soup simmering before him, he paid them no heed. Frank pulled up behind him. The cook was holding a wooden spoonful of soup up to his mouth, blowing and sipping on it, holding his left hand under the spoon to catch the drippings.

"Benson," said Frank. "We want to talk to you."

"Not right now, boss," said Benson, frowning in concentration as he reached for a salt shaker.

"Goddammit, Benson! Drop that fucking spoon!"

Benson put down the spoon and turned to face Frank.

"Who's down here with you?" Frank demanded.

"Jimmy and Raz."

Frank looked to his right. Raz, a thin, stringy black man was carefully dumping a sack of onions into one of the deep sinks. Beyond him at the chopping table, Jimmy Parker was slicing a gleaming pile of filet mignon into butterfly cuts for the night's special. Parker's ruined face looked like a baked apple. He was whistling softly as he worked, and for a change appeared to be cold sober.

Frank looked back at Benson. "Where's Ahmed? I thought he was down here, too."

"He left."

"How come?"

"He wasn't feelin' so hot. I let him go home for a while. We can't afford no sickness in the kitchen, Frank."

Frank looked around at his two stooges. "Did you look everywhere in this kitchen?"

"Sure Frank," Luigi said. "Ask Benson."

"That's right, Frank," said the cook. "I was here when they came in. I saw them. They looked everywhere."

"Show me." Frank said. "Show me where they looked."

"Jesus, Frank, I can't leave this soup. It's today's soup du jour!"

"I don't give a fuck what it is. Turn it off."

"But that would ruin it." The man was practically in tears.

"Show me around this kitchen," Frank told him, "or I'll dump the whole fucking pot over your silly head."

Benson lost interest in the soup du jour and led them around behind the stove, crossing in front of the six new G.E. microwaves lined up eye level on metal shelves along the wall. Benson had been after Frank to get the ovens since he first took the job. A month ago Frank got a call from the don, telling him the ovens were on the way, part of a trailer load they'd boosted outside Jersey City. The fact that Carmine himself had called to tell him about it had been a good sign. But unless Frank got his ass out of this particular sling, there would be no more such good signs in the future.

They walked into the huge pantry, and when they

came out, Luigi led them past the walk-in freezer toward the three deep cast-iron sinks alongside the swing doors that opened onto the loading platform.

"Hold it," said Frank.

The three men halted.

"What about that meat cooler we just passed?" Frank looked at Luigi. "Did you look in there?"

"Jesus, no, Frank," Luigi said. "How could she get in there? And if she locked herself in, she'd freeze her fuckin' boobs off."

"I already told you. She had help."

Turning and walking back to the cooler, Frank pulled open the door. The cold air chilled him, and as he stepped inside, he could see his breath. He switched on the light. Wrapped in gleaming plastic, plucked chickens and ducks hung from the steel racks. Farther in, Frank glimpsed the sides of beef, pork ribs, ham hocks, and the grisly coils of sausages, gleaming like a man's spilled guts.

"Hey," said Benson.

Frank turned. Benson was looking at an empty hook by the freezer door.

"What's wrong?"

"I always keep an old fur coat hanging on this hook," Benson said. "Case I have to do some quick cutting in here. It's gone."

Frank stormed past Benson and out of the cooler, the rest following. A beat-up cunt with half her clothes ripped off would need that fur coat to keep herself from freezing. As Benson slammed shut the cooler door, Frank turned on him.

"You say it was just you and Ahmed down here?"

BODY PARTS

"Sure, boss."

"Did you dump her in there, Benson?"

"Me? Jesus, Frank. What're you sayin'?"

"That's right. I forgot about that soup du jour. You wouldn't have the time. When did Ahmed leave?"

"About an hour ago."

"He went home, did he?"

"That's what he told me, Frank."

"Were you with him all the time you two were in here?"

Benson hesitated. "Most of the time."

"What's that supposed to mean?"

"I left the kitchen to chase some teenagers messin' with my Fiero."

"You seen them kids yourself?"

"No. Ahmed did."

"And he was the one told you about 'em. Right?"

"Yeah, Frank. As a matter of fact, he did."

Frank felt a quick build of elation. Now he had Mary Lou—and the nigger bastard who'd helped her.

"Just tell me where that black son of a bitch lives."

Benson gave Frank Ahmed's address, his eyes wide, obviously wondering what in the hell this was all about. But Frank told him nothing as he left the kitchen and led Luigi and Moon out onto the loading platform.

"We'll take your car," Frank told Moon.

The three jumped to the ground and crunched over the gravel. Frank glanced at his wristwatch, wondering what in the hell was keeping Caesar. These two fuck-ups weren't worth diddly-shit.

CHAPTER 7

On his way down Greentree Road, Skip saw the Trans Am leave Violi's parking lot and head toward him. He cut swiftly into a residential driveway, waited for the Trans Am to pass, then made a U-turn, jouncing through a patch of shrubbery, and took after it.

The Trans Am circled the lake and drove back into Lake Placid, coming to a halt on a side street across from a small park. The Neanderthal and the dago, along with an older, darkly handsome mob type, got out and entered a rundown brick apartment building. FORTY-ONE HUCKLEBERRY STREET was etched in the weathered concrete arch over its entrance. The older man, Skip figured, was the Frank Santorini who now managed Violi's restaurant.

Skip parked a few doors down and leaned back against his seat, considering his options.

He didn't have many.

From what Violet had told him, the Neanderthal and the dago already had Mary Lou, which meant they were probably holding her in that building somewhere, and what they sure as hell would want to know from her was who the fuck *he* was. Looked at from their angle, he *had* to be a confederate of hers. How else could he have known where she had stashed that insurance policy? Meanwhile, Mary Lou would have no idea who they were talking about or how he had managed to liberate those four keys; only it wasn't very likely they'd take her word when she denied knowing anything about him.

All this meant she was in for a beating, Skip concluded—or worse—unless he walked in and cleared things up, made a deal, maybe.

He left his car and walked down to 41 Huckleberry. Pushing through the unlocked vestibule door, he paused at the foot of the stairs, his hand on the railing. The sharp odor of urine-saturated diapers filled the first-floor hall. Through the apartment doors came the mutter of several TV sets, making for a discordant clash of voices, laugh tracks, and music. And from an apartment at the end of the hall came an infant's wail, steady and unrelenting.

He ascended the stairs. On the second floor landing he paused. From a nearby apartment, a ghetto

BODY PARTS

blaster throbbed. Farther down the hall, above the blaster's steady, mindless beat, came the idiot rush of canned laughter. He continued on up to the third-floor landing and heard a girl's frightened, pleading voice. He walked toward the sound and came to the last apartment in the dank hallway. The lock had been forced, and the door was slightly ajar. He nudged it open all the way and stepped inside, then paused to listen as the girl's protests clashed with a male's heavy, threatening voice.

Skip pulled the door shut behind him and walked softly down the hall, aware of a sharp odor of turpentine. He passed an unoccupied living room and heard ahead of him the ugly, unmistakable thud of a clenched fist striking flesh, followed by a shrill, protesting squeal of pain from the girl. The defiant protest he caught in her voice told him she was not submitting easily. He reached an open doorway leading into a small bedroom and stepped through it.

The dago and Frank Santorini were standing at the foot of the bed. Startled, they flung about to face him. Leaning over the girl on the bed, the Neanderthal's upraised right fist froze in midair. They had hung a young black man from a nail driven into the closet's door frame. A wire coat hanger was twisted around his neck, and his arms were belted to his side. He was sweating bullets and his eyes were shut tightly in concentration. But he wasn't dead yet because his feet could just reach the floor. Mary Lou was huddled against the bed's headboard, hugging her knees protectively, tears streaking down her battered face.

Bill Knott

Confused, the Neanderthal looked quickly at Santorini, then straightened and lowered his fist.

Skip lifted a wooden chair away from the wall and planted it beside the bed. He nudged his hat back off his forehead and sat down, folding his arms over the back of the chair as if this were a public pool hall or gym and he had just strolled in to watch the action.

Santorini and the dago were as nonplussed as the Neanderthal. Through her tears, Mary Lou Dobbs stared wide-eyed at Skip.

"Who the fuck are you, mister?" Santorini demanded in the same heavy, threatening voice Skip had heard him use questioning the girl.

Skip handed him his business card. Santorini glanced at it, looked at Skip in pure amazement, then grinned and pocketed the card.

"So *you're* the repo man."

Skip nodded.

"You some kind of nut, walkin' in like this?"

"If this girl here is Mary Lou Dobbs, I have business with her."

"What kind of business?"

"You have my card. Mary Lou has failed to make payments on a very expensive Lamborghini the Mohawk Adjustment Service has been hired to repossess."

Santorini, triumphant, glanced at the dago.

"Well, Luigi? Is this the repo man you numbskulls lost on the way back here?"

"Yeah, Frank. That's him, all right."

"That's right, Frank," the Neanderthal agreed eagerly, eyes lighting as he looked over Skip. "He's the one took them kilos from Mary Lou's place."

Santorini looked back at Skip. "Don't tell me, repo man. You want to deal."

"You got it, Frank."

"Name it."

"The Lamborghini for the nose candy."

"A straight switch, you mean?"

Skip nodded.

"That's all you want, the car for the coke?"

"It takes a while, but you do catch on."

Santorini glanced at the Neanderthal. "All right, Moon. Take a rest. And let Ahmed down. Looks like we got what we came here for."

Moon reached up, lifted the black off the nail, and flung him across the foot of the bed. The hanger went flying. The black, gasping for breath, his arms still strapped tightly, collapsed facedown onto the rumpled bedspread. Mary Lou Dobbs, still staring in amazement at Skip, pushed herself farther up against the headboard.

"Can we talk someplace else?" Skip asked.

"Sure," Santorini said. "In the other room here."

With Luigi keeping close behind Skip, Skip followed Frank Santorini down the hall into the living room. Textbooks were piled carelessly against one wall. A few had spilled into a corner where they lay amidst empty beer cans and Coke bottles. On the floor in front of the sofa, discarded dirty socks had grown rigid. The air in the room was rank with the stench of soiled underwear.

Pushing aside an empty Domino Pizza box, Skip

slumped down onto a partially disemboweled Naugahyde sofa. Santorini sat carefully in a crooked recliner. Luigi remained on his feet to one side of his boss, keeping an eye on Skip.

"So okay," Santorini said, "you're sayin' all you want for them kilos is the Lamborghini. Right?"

"I have what you want, you have what I want."

"You sayin' you ain't been in this with Mary Lou from the beginning?"

"I never saw the girl before in my life."

"I don't know," Santorini said. "That's pretty hard to believe. And besides that, this looks too damned easy. How do I know you ain't working with the feds?"

"You got any idea how long they would tie up that Lamborghini once they connected it to drug trafficking—and that chain-saw massacre in the motel?"

"Yeah, yeah. I can see that." Then Santorini leaned forward suddenly. "Say, listen. You been there? I mean to the motel? You seen what Moon did?"

"I saw."

"Pretty messy, huh?"

"Where the hell did you pick up that Neanderthal, Frank? He ought to be in a cage."

Santorini glanced uneasily into the bedroom. "Look, I didn't have no idea he'd take that ax with him. So help me. I just wanted him and Luigi to bring in Mary Lou. She called me from the motel, told me she'd brought up one of them crazy Colombians to protect her—said if I didn't spring for the car, she'd go to my wife and start bugling. So I sent Moon over there with Luigi here to get her. How did I know he was going to go apeshit?"

"All right. So you didn't know. I'll buy that. But right now, Frank, what I want is that car."

Santorini sat back in the recliner. "You're a cool one, you are. All business. Well, hell, I can appreciate that. You want to deal, we deal. The Lamborghini for the four keys. A straight swap. I like it. Except for one thing."

"What's that?"

"I want to believe you, repo man. I really do. Hell, you're doing me a favor. You're makin' it easy for me. But if you weren't in this thing with Mary Lou from the start, how'd you know where she'd stashed them four kilos?"

"Her old lady told me."

"How come?"

"It's like this, Frank. I went to her place looking for the car, and her old lady and I got to talking. She said Mary Lou was coming back later for her insurance, which was the first time Mary Lou had ever mentioned insurance to her. So I put two and two together, searched her bedroom, then the john. The coke was stashed behind the tank."

Santorini glanced at Luigi.

Luigi nodded. "Yeah, Frank. That's where she told us she put it."

Santorini looked back at Skip. "Okay, so maybe I'll buy your story."

"Where's the Lamborghini, Frank?"

"We got it hid."

"Where?"

Santorini laughed. "It's in a safe place. Don't worry. You don't think I'm dumb enough to tell you where it is before I get what I'm after, do you?"

"All right then. Deliver the Lamborghini to your restaurant. When I'm behind the wheel, I'll hand out the four kilos to you."

Santorini considered Skip's proposal for a minute or so, then shook his head. "I don't like it, repo man."

"Why not?"

"What's to stop you from handing me pure shit, then flooring the accelerator?"

Skip shrugged. "What do you suggest?"

"Bring them kilos to my restaurant tonight. Have a meal on the house. Try the fettuccine Alfredo while I test the goods. When I'm satisfied it's the genuine article, I'll give the word and Luigi here will bring around the Lamborghini."

"Sounds reasonable," Skip said. Then he smiled at Santorini. "Just don't try anything stupid."

"Hey," said Frank, raising both hands, palms out. "We're partners."

Skip got to his feet. "What time do we meet at the restaurant?"

"Suit yourself."

"Eight-thirty."

"Fine."

"The fettuccini Alfredo, you say?"

"Try it. Believe me, it's the best in the north country."

On his way out, Skip ducked his head into the bedroom. Mary Lou Dobbs, eyes dry now, was cradling the black in her arms. Moon was sitting in a white wicker chair, watching them. He reminded Frank of a hungry dog on a tight leash, his food dish just out of reach.

When Skip reached the door, he turned to Santorini and Luigi.

"Don't try to follow me when I drive away from here. Do that and the deal's off. And that Lamborghini better be in apple pie order when your boy here brings it around tonight."

"Don't worry, repo man," Frank assured him. "You just keep your end of the deal."

Skip drove down the first side street he came to and kept on around the block, looking for a spot to park where his decal would not stand out. He came finally to a Super Duper food market, swung into its lot, parked in the midst of the shoppers' cars and walked back to Huckleberry Street. He stepped into a doorway a few buildings down from Forty-one and was just in time to see Santorini and the other two leave the building and drive off. There was no one else with them. Which meant they had left Mary Lou and the black alone up there in the apartment.

He didn't like that, which was why he had come back. There was no telling what Santorini would do to them now that he figured they were no longer needed.

Alive.

Skip hurried into the building and climbed to the

third floor. He pushed open the sagging door and hurried into the bedroom. Mary Lou was strapped to the bed, a wide strip of tape over her mouth. The black was hanging from the nail again, his feet propped precariously onto the back of the wicker chair. His face was glistening with sweat, and when he saw Skip in the doorway, he almost let his foot slip off the chair. Skip stepped quickly into the room, lifted Ahmed off the nail and dropped him into the wicker chair, then unbuckled the belt holding down his arms. The black slumped back in the chair and flung the wire hanger across the room.

"Oh, man," he gasped. "I'm sure glad you came back."

"I returned as soon as I could," he said, bending over Mary Lou.

"Them bastards!" she cried, the words exploding in the room the moment Skip removed the tape.

Skip untied her bound hands and unstrapped her from the bed.

"They laughed at me," she fumed, sitting up. "They knew I never could've got free. They wanted me to lay here and watch Ahmed hang himself! Oh, them fucking bastards!"

"Not nice people, I admit," said Skip.

"And you just walked right in and sat down with them," she panted. "Like it was nothing, what they were doing. Who the hell are you, mister?"

"Name's Tracewski," he told her. "I'm up here to repossess that Lamborghini. Like that poor sap you took to the motel. You remember him, do you? Jimmy Vasquez."

BODY PARTS

"Oh, God," she groaned, suddenly contrite. "Yes, I remember him. Jesus. How could I ever forget?"

Ahmed sat down on the bed beside Mary Lou and put his arm around her. She leaned her head back against his shoulder, apparently recalling all too vividly what had happened to Jimmy Vasquez.

Skip saw an ax leaning against the wall next to the closet, its blade and most of the handle dark with dried blood. It hadn't been there when he entered before. Neat. They'd brought it up and set it there. He didn't think he needed to ask, but he did so anyway.

"Who does that ax belong to?"

"Moon," Ahmed said. "Frank sent him down to his car for it. He figured when they found me dead, they'd find the ax that killed your man right next to me and the case would be closed."

Skip nodded. It might have worked. Filled with remorse for the terrible crime he had committed in a wild, jealous rage, Mary Lou's black lover had been unable to face life any longer. Not bad as far as it went, but it didn't go far enough. Frank still had to account for Mary Lou. Which meant he'd soon be sending someone over to finish her off. Her death by an O.D. maybe, sprawled on the floor beside her man, would be the last crude, effective touch. A twentieth century Romeo and Juliet, and nobody would want to dig into it any deeper.

"You two better get yourselves together," Skip told them. "Then haul ass."

"You think Frank's coming back?" Ahmed asked.

Bill Knott

"Him or someone else."

"Why?"

"To finish off Mary Lou."

"Hell, I ain't waitin' here for that," Mary Lou cried, jumping to her feet. "Only first I got to take a whiz and clean myself off."

Ahmed followed after her in the direction of the bathroom, looking as urgent as Mary Lou.

Drawn by the smell of turpentine and linseed oil, Skip stepped into the adjoining room and found what passed for Ahmed's studio. It was a chaotic mess. Batman and girly posters attached with Scotch tape peeled off the walls. The woodwork was stained with oil paint, the bare wooden floor discolored from discarded tubes of oil paint that had been ground into it. A few of Ahmed's unfinished paintings were leaning against the walls; others rested in an untidy pile in one corner.

The unfinished painting on the easel was of a mountain glen with peaks towering in the distance. A typical Adirondack scene.

It was awful.

What riveted Skip from the outset was Ahmed's unnaturally bright blue sky and white clouds, the grass and trees a thick, uniform green. A lake in the foreground was as blue as the sky above it, the perspective so poorly drawn that the lake looked like a dinner plate standing on end.

Skip returned to the bedroom as Mary Lou and Ahmed entered it. She had combed out her hair and looked a little better, though her bruised face was still a mess. He wondered how she could see out of her eyes, the ridges were so swollen.

"Where are you two going now?" Skip asked.

Mary Lou shrugged.

"Me," said Ahmed, sitting down on the bed, "I'm goin' home—back to Detroit."

Mary Lou looked at him in surprise. "Detroit?"

"You heard me, little mother. Detroit. Fuck this bein' an artist, paintin' pictures and working for minimum wage in that white devil's kitchen. I got to get me to a higher standard of livin'—even if I do die young."

"What'll you do in Detroit?" Skip asked.

"Good steady work, man. Make deliveries to the body shops south of Detroit. Caddies, Lincoln town cars, BMWs, whatever they want."

"How are you going to get there?"

"My van's downstairs."

"Ahmed, I want to go with you," Mary Lou said.

"You crazy? You wanta leave this lovely country—leave all your honky friends behind?"

"I don't have no friends here, Ahmed. Not anymore I don't."

"What about that expensive condo in Miami?"

"I don't think Frank'll let me keep it now, not after what I done—coming back like this."

"What about your mother?" Skip asked.

Mary Lou shrugged. "Ma'll be all right. She won't miss me none. Never did know I was around. All she knows is what's goin' on inside that tube. She's got her welfare check and the winter oil check and the house is all paid for."

Bill Knott

"Violet's in deep clover, then."

She smiled wanly at Skip. "Looks that way, don't it?"

Skip glanced at Ahmed. "It's up to you."

Ahmed surveyed the battered Mary Lou. "We travel light, little mother—and we leave now."

"I'm ready," Mary Lou told him. "Let's go."

"There's just one little hitch. I need gas money."

"I got some."

"How much?"

She smiled. It was ghastly to see what that did to her discolored features. "Don't worry. It's enough. Maybe more than enough. I didn't spend all that money Frank gave me, and I hid it in a good place."

"Little mother," Ahmed said, standing up, "it's time we split from this cold north country."

Skip grabbed the ax, put his hat on and followed them out of the apartment and down the stairs. He bid them good-bye as they climbed into the van, then watched them drive off. Keeping the ax out of sight under his overcoat, he walked back to the Super Duper parking lot, locked the ax in the Mazda's trunk, and drove back to the Thunderbird.

The desk clerk handed Skip a message that had been waiting for him. Skip unfolded the slip of paper and read that a Miss Terry Lindsay had called and would appreciate a return call.

Up in his room he dialed Terry's number and leaned his head back on the bed's pillow.

"Are we still on speaking terms?" she asked.

"I'm returning your call, so I assume we are."

BODY PARTS

"I know it sounds silly, Skip—but sometimes I get the feeling you're deliberately trying to make it difficult for us."

"Now why," he asked wearily, "would I want to do that?"

She hesitated before replying. "So I'll be the one who breaks it off."

"You're right. You're being silly."

"Am I?"

"Yes, you are," he replied, realizing she would not believe him and that there was no way in God's green earth he could convince her otherwise. And that the moment he tried to do so, he was dead. She'd got this notion in her head, and was determined to run with it.

"Skip . . . ?"

"I'm still here."

"I'm off now—and I managed a weekend free. I could make it up there in a few hours. We could be together."

"Terry, I'm chasing all over hell and beyond to find that Lamborghini. We'd have little chance to be together."

"Maybe I could help you find it."

"I'm sorry, Terry, but I got to go now."

He hung up and left his room, so if she called back, he wouldn't be there to answer.

Following the desk clerk's directions, he found a small luggage store a few blocks down from the motel and bought a blue overnight bag that bore a close resemblance to Mary Lou's. On his way back he stopped into a supermarket and purchased a four-pound sack of granulated sugar and a box of Baggies.

Back in his room he opened both suitcases. Into the one he had just bought, he transferred about half of Mary Lou's undies and blouses, then filled nine Baggies with sugar and nudged them carefully in under Mary Lou's things. Placing a Baggie of the good stuff on top, he closed the suitcase. The other overnight bag, the one containing the rest of the coke, he took downstairs and gave to the desk clerk, asking him to put it into the motel safe for him.

"One more thing," he told the clerk, slipping him a ten. "Anyone comes in here looking for me, I want him to call my room first. I don't want any surprises."

"Sure thing, Mr. Tracewski."

Skip returned to his room, picked up the other blue suitcase, went back downstairs and tossed it onto the backseat of his car. Then he drove out of the lot.

"Is that you, Carmen?" Carlotta asked.

"No, it ain't. This here is Carmine DiAngelo."

"It's about Frank."

"Frank who, dammit!"

"Frank Santorini. Don't you remember, Carmen?"

"Car*mine*. I ain't no dame. Car*mine!* Who the hell is this?"

"It's Carlotta. Don't you remember me, Carmine?"

His voice went a notch lower. "Hey, you a friend or something? I meet you someplace, maybe?"

"Yes, of course. At Frank's wedding. Surely, you remember? After the ceremonies you took me aside and told me if I ever needed your help I should just give you a call."

"Frank's wedding?" There was a pause, and then, "Oh, yeah! Sure! Frank's wedding! You're Carlotta. I remember."

"Carmine, Frank's been very mean lately."

"That so?"

"I wouldn't have called you otherwise."

"Well, I'm sure sorry to hear that. Say, listen, Carlotta, you caught me at a bad time. I got some business here right now. Maybe you should call me back later, huh?"

"No," Carlotta said, suddenly hurt and angry all over again. "I need to talk to you right now. I've had a terrible time getting hold of you."

"Okay. Okay. So what happened?"

"Frank struck me!"

"What's that?"

"Frank hit me with his fist! He's a wife beater, Carmine."

"That so, huh? You two have a quarrel?"

"Why, of course! Do you imagine Frank would hit me for no reason? Certainly we had a quarrel."

"Look, Carlotta—Frank, he's an excitable guy. I mean, he's really got a fiery temperament, see. So maybe you shouldn't put no stock in what he done. After all, what's one belt? That ain't goin' to kill you.

Bill Knott

I tell you what. Cook him up a nice batch of spaghetti and meat balls and he'll warm right up to you."

"I am *not* going to cook him up a batch of spaghetti! Not after what he just did to me. And I want him to sell that restaurant."

"Sell it? Jesus! Why should he do that, Carlotta?" For the first time Carmine sounded really concerned.

"Well, I . . . been hearing things."

His voice dropped a notch lower. "What things?"

She could tell Carmine was interested now, and she wanted to keep him that way, keep him concerned. "There's been talk about . . . drugs. I overheard someone say that if you want good quality Peruvian flake, you should go to Violi's. What's Peruvian flake, Carmine? Isn't that illegal drugs?"

"What else you been hearin', Carlotta?"

"Well . . . this is *very* personal, Carmine. And I did not want to bring it up. But there's been talk of him and a young blond girl who was a hostess in the restaurant—and also talk that Frank bought her a very expensive car. A Lamborghini, I think, a white Lamborghini. But, of course, I don't really believe such talk. I'm sure its all gossip."

"Hey, thatsa girl, Carlotta. You're right. You shouldn't oughta believe what them crazy people tell you. Frank's a good boy. Only like I said, he's maybe a little excitable at times."

"Oh, he certainly is, Carmine. I guess it must be his fiery Mediterranean temperament, as you say. And I do feel much better now that I've talked to you. You're so understanding. I'm sorry to bother you like this, but I just didn't know who else to turn to."

"Hey, listen. You did right calling me, Carlotta. You wait a minute now, huh? I gotta talk to someone."

Carlotta waited, afraid she might have gone too far in revealing this malicious gossip, for until Frank's outburst, she had refused to believe a word of it, telling herself it was just the product of baseless jealousy. She was only too well aware of how much the women in her circle lusted after her handsome Italian husband.

"Listen, Carlotta," Carmine said, coming back on the phone. "I think it stinks, Frank treating you like that. I think maybe I should have a word with the crazy bastard. Calm him down some."

"You mean you'll call him?"

"Better than that. I'll drive up there and have a heart to heart talk with him."

"Oh, Carmine, *would* you?" She was delighted.

"Only don't say nothin' to Frank. I want it to be a surprise. You unnerstan' what I'm sayin'?"

"Certainly. I won't say a word. And Carmine, I can't thank you enough. I'm sure once Frank has a talk with you, he'll become once again that fine Italian gentleman I love so much."

"Yeah, sure, Carlotta. Just remember what I said now. Don't let on to Frank you called me, and don't tell him I'm coming up." He paused for emphasis. "Like I said, I want it to be a surprise."

"Oh, I won't tell him a thing, Carmine. That's a

promise. And I'm sure Frank will be so glad to see you. It'll be a lovely surprise."

"Yeah. That's right, Carlotta."

She said good-bye and hung up, feeling much, much better.

CHAPTER 8

Skip walked into Violi's lounge and, shrugging out of his topcoat, lowered himself onto a bar stool. He folded the topcoat carefully on the stool next to him and placed his snap-brim hat on top of it. At the other end of the bar a town cop wearing wraparound sunglasses was hunched over a cup of coffee, deep in conversation with the bartender. The grip of his .38 Police Special stuck out ominously from his black leather holster. Skip glanced at the bartender, but the man avoided eye contact with him as he continued his conversation. Skip gave up and glanced about the place. In a corner booth, a Phyllis Diller type in an orange fright wig was pushing her wares on a nervous elderly gentleman with watery eyes and a slight tremor.

Violi's Italian Restaurant and Lounge depressed Skip.

Cooled fitfully by a rattling air conditioner, the air was fetid with stale cigarette smoke and the faint but insistent smell of sweaty armpits and K mart perfume. The bar's dominant color scheme was black with red trim, with indirect lighting over the red leather booths. Tacky silver musical notes had been Scotch-taped onto the bandstand's black skirt, and a glass-beaded curtain hung in the archway separating the bar from the restaurant's main dining room. A blue light beam on the ceiling was focused on the beaded curtain to highlight its flashing gleam whenever anyone clattered through it. Looking at the sparkling beads, Skip found himself waiting for Milton Caniff's Dragon Lady to part them and step through, pause a moment while every eye in the place swiveled in her direction, then stride sulkily toward him.

He sighed inwardly. No such luck.

Convinced finally that Skip was not going to give up and stomp out of the bar, the bartender pulled back from the cop and headed toward him.

"What'll it be?"

"Coors. On tap, if you've got it."

The bartender shook his head with heavy finality. "We ain't got no Coors on tap. All we got's Miller's." It sounded like a challenge.

"Done."

BODY PARTS

The bartender filled a stein and planted it down on a napkin in front of Skip, the suds skidding down the side of the glass. Skip put two bills on the bar. The bartender grabbed them, rang up the sale, and slapped Skip's change down in front of him. Then he ducked through an open door behind him to the back room. In a moment Skip heard the thump of wooden cases being moved about along with the cheerful clink of bottles.

He stepped down from his stool and, pushing his beer along the bar, joined the cop.

"How you doin', officer?"

The cop turned slowly to contemplate Skip, his eyes hidden by the cheaters, and Skip caught the intended menace the man projected. From his own years on the Albany force, he found no difficulty imagining this cop's history. A schoolyard and neighborhood bully, he had grown up and made a wise career choice.

"You got a problem, mister?"

"Problem?" Skip replied. "Me? Why, not at all. Just thought I'd join you in a drink. You off duty now?"

The cop indicated his uniform with a flick of his chin. "Does it look like it?"

"Just wondered." Skip sipped his beer. "Figured you'd be the man to ask. Since I'm not too familiar with this here lovely town of yours."

"Ask me what?"

"You consider this a nice place to bring up kids?"

The cop frowned, obviously wondering if Skip was for real. "Yeah, I guess. Why not?"

"Well, now," Skip said, brightening hopefully, "that's just what I was hoping to hear—and coming from a police officer, it makes it all the more reassuring. I mean, you'd be the first to know if there was any illicit drugs, back-room gambling . . . unlawful goings on like that. Because I was thinkin' of moving up here—away from the big city, if you get my meaning."

The cop peered at him through his Darth Vader windows. "Where you from?"

"Albany."

"Hell, that's not a bad place."

"It is if you want to bring your kids up in a decent God-fearing environment, like up here in this beautiful country."

The cop looked away. "Yeah, sure."

"You know this town pretty well, huh?"

"I guess."

"Saw some lovely homes driving in."

"That so?"

"Yeah. Wondered what places like that go for up here."

"You mean them on the hill behind the golf course?"

"That's right. Off Route 73."

"No, them ain't off 73," he said, irritated at Skip's stupidity. "The golf course is off Route 12."

"Oh, yeah. That's right. That's the one I meant. Them houses on the hill. Very nice."

"They ain't cheap."

"I understand Mr. Santorini lives up there."

BODY PARTS

Vaguely suspicious, the cop turned his head to regard Skip more closely.

"You know Frank?"

"Oh sure. Great guy. Whenever I'm in town, I eat here, and he's been nice enough to stop by my table to say hello. A fine man. Makes you realize what nonsense all that talk about the mafia is. It was Frank himself pointed out what a lovely town this is."

"What do you do for a livin', mister?"

"Me? I'm with Kemper Insurance. Liability, mostly."

The cop turned back to his coffee and sipped it.

"Say," Skip said, reaching into a side pocket as if he were going to dig out his business card, "now that you mention it, would you by any chance be interested in one of our policies?"

The cop quickly, emphatically, shook his head. "No way, mister. The town's already got us a good policy. I don't need no insurance. I'm all set."

"Well, I'm sure that's a great comfort to you."

"Yeah."

"Anyway, like I was sayin', I figure if a man as important as Mr. Santorini lives in that neighborhood, it might be a good spot for me to locate, too."

"You mean up on Golf Course Road?"

"I thought I saw a house for sale up there as I drove past."

The cop shrugged. "Maybe so. But all them places on that hill are pretty steep."

"Worth it, though. Spectacular view. And all that fresh air. The children would love it."

Bill Knott

"Yeah." The cop glanced down the bar, obviously hoping the barkeep would return. He had no desire to continue this nothing conversation with a downstate insurance salesman, and he was hoping for another cup of Irish coffee. But the barkeep was still busy in the back room. Giving up, the cop downed the last of his coffee, pushed away from the bar and, without a word to Skip, lumbered heavily toward the outside door.

"Nice talkin' to you," Skip called after him.

"Yeah."

The cop pushed open the door and vanished into the afternoon sun's bright glare.

The bartender returned, lugging a case of Carling's Ale. As he set it down on the runway he glanced up and met Skip's smiling glance.

"Any chance of a sandwich to go with this beer?" Skip asked.

"The kitchen's closed."

"Just a ham and cheese would be all I'd want now."

"Hey, didn't I just tell you, mister? The kitchen's closed. It don't open till four."

"No need to get nasty about it."

"You got a complaint, see the man runs the place."

"Frank?"

"Yeah. Go on up and make your beef. I'm busy."

Skip shrugged and sipped his beer. "Just a ham and cheese. Hell, I could go on into the kitchen and make it myself."

The bartender was about to respond but gave up the idea and began lifting bottles out of the case and placing them down in the ice chest under the bar. The outside door opened. Skip turned to see a short, bald, powerfully-built man walk in. Coming from the bright sunlight outside, he had to pause a moment to accustom his eyes to the gloom before he walked over to the bar and stood quietly with his hands on the edge of it, waiting for the bartender to look up. At last he did.

"Frank in?"

"Who're you?"

"Give me a beer and go tell him Caesar's here."

"You tell him yourself, mister. I ain't no messenger boy."

The little man looked at the bartender for a long moment, his stiletto eyes cold and unblinking. "I think maybe you don't hear me," he said softly. "Give me a beer, then go tell Frank what I said."

Something clicked deep inside the bartender's meager comprehension, and he realized suddenly what manner of man he was dealing with. Cold sweat stood out on his brow. With amazing alacrity he swung about, drew the beer Caesar had requested, and wiping his hands on his apron, plunged around the bar and disappeared through the beaded curtain.

Caesar lifted the beer and drank greedily, emptying the stein in a few quick gulps. Grinning, Skip caught his eye and lifted his own beer in salute.

"Cheers, mister. That's tellin' the sonofabitch. Have one on me."

"That's all right," Caesar said. "I don't pay here."

Skip finished his drink and pushed away from the

Bill Knott

bar. He glanced over at the corner booth and saw that Phyllis Diller had left already with that old coot. More power to them both. He put on his hat, shrugged into his topcoat, and with a cheery wave to Caesar, pushed out through the door, squinting as he walked through the glare to his car.

Skip braked quietly on the gravel driveway in front of Frank Santorini's three-car garage. At least he was reasonably certain this was where Santorini lived, since it was by far the most palatial of the homes on Golf Course Drive. All three garage doors were down, he noticed. He got out of the Mazda and stared at the garage for a moment, then walked over to intercept a gardener pushing a wheelbarrow loaded with sifted potting soil toward a distant line of hedges. The lawn stretching between the gravel drive and the hedges was as carefully manicured as a golf course. When Skip reached him, the gardener halted and took off his mud-streaked Yankee baseball cap and wiped his brow with the back of his hand.

"Can I help you, mister?"

"This here the Santorini place? I didn't see any mailbox at the drive's entrance."

The raw-boned old man, probably in his early sixties, was tanned almost black from the sun. "Yep, this is where Mr. Santorini lives," he said carefully.

Skip gazed around at the well-kept grounds. "I got to admit it. You sure do keep this place nice."

His eyes gleamed with a sudden pride. "Yep. It keeps me busy."

"I'll just go up and knock on the door," Skip said.

"You lookin' for the missus?"

"Mrs. Santorini, yes."

"Carlotta ain't in the house. She's around back in the arboretum."

"The what?"

He clapped his Yankee hat on, lifted the wheelbarrow's handles and started toward the hedges. "Arboretum. Least, that's what she calls it."

"Much obliged."

Circling the sprawling house with its innumerable wings and hedge-bordered flower gardens took a while. But he eventually came upon Carlotta Santorini reclining on a chaise longue on a flagstone patio which was surrounded by tiers of hedges, flowers, and young pines, providing an almost impenetrable screen about the patio. Carlotta's hair was combed out and she had on a long pink housecoat with lace flounces up the front and along the hem. She had not buttoned her housecoat all the way up, and since she was wearing nothing under it, he caught a generous glimpse of her cleft. She was not a pretty woman; her jawline was too long, her eyes slightly protuberant.

She was reading a fashion magazine and did not hear him approaching over the thick carpet of grass. He paused and coughed to indicate his presence. She sat up at once and looked in his direction. Smiling, he continued on toward her.

Bill Knott

She got up from the chaise longue, obviously discomfited by his intrusion.

"Yes . . . ?"

"Don't worry, Mrs. Santorini," he assured her, smiling. "I'm not an encyclopedia salesman."

"If it's my husband you wish to see, he's—"

Skip handed her his business card. She glanced at it, then handed it back to him, frowning. "But I don't understand, Mr. Tracewski. You repossess vehicles. That is, you take them back from people who don't pay. Am I correct?"

"Yes."

"Then there must be some mistake. Both my husband's car and my own are paid for."

"It's not your car I'm after." Skip took off his coat and began fanning himself with his hat. "Would you mind if I sat down? It's been a long day."

"Oh, of course. Forgive me. Sit down, by all means. Would you care for something to drink?"

"Nothing special," he said, sitting in one of the white metal chairs drawn up around the patio's glass-topped table. "A glass of water would be fine."

"A soft drink?"

"You got some Coke, maybe?"

"I'm sure we do."

Excusing herself, she left him and walked back across the flagstones to the house. She slid aside the glass door and he heard her call out to someone called Jane. The second time she had to shout. A black woman with an apron on and a broom in her hand appeared. Carlotta spoke to her softly and returned to Skip. He noticed that while she had had

BODY PARTS

her back to him, she had buttoned her housedress, and when she sat down on the chaise longue, she was careful to cover her long bony legs.

Sitting this close to her, Skip saw clearly the dark bruise on the side of her chin. She had done her best to hide it with makeup. Her eyes were slightly bloodshot—from recent tears, he surmised.

"If it's not one of our cars you're after, Mr. Tracewski," she said, "just how can I help you?"

Skip hesitated. He was reluctant to cause this woman any additional grief. It was clear that not too long before, Frank Santorini had already taken a few punishing swipes at her.

"Well," he began reluctantly, "it's not your car or your husband's I'm after."

"Oh?"

"I'm looking for the car Mr. Santorini bought in Florida."

"In Florida?"

"Yes—a Lamborghini."

Jane stepped out onto the patio with a tray containing two tall glasses of Coca-Cola. Skip waited for the woman to bring over the drinks. Jane held the tray as Carlotta took her glass, then set the tray down on the table in front of Skip.

Skip thanked her as he lifted his glass off the tray. Jane returned to the house.

"Did you say . . . a Lamborghini?" Carlotta asked, staring at Skip. She was paying no attention to the glass in her hand.

"Yes. A *white* Lamborghini, to be exact."

"That's . . . one of those terrribly fast European cars, isn't it?"

Skip nodded and took a sip of the Coke. "Very low to the ground, very fast, and very, *very* expensive. Gull doors that swing up, and it has a wing on the rear deck. The wing on this one's been removed."

She put her drink down untouched on a flagstone beside her chair. "Surely, if Frank owned such a car he'd be driving it. He drives a Jaguar—a birthday present from me."

"Well, the thing is, he didn't buy it for himself."

"What do you mean?" Her voice was suddenly very small.

"He bought it for a local girl, a Mary Lou Dobbs. Only he didn't finish paying for it. Yesterday I sent one of my men to pick up the car and he ran into some bad trouble. I suppose it will be on the evening news tonight."

"Why, what do you mean? What happened to this man?"

"He was murdered, Mrs. Santorini. Brutally. And the car was taken."

She closed her eyes and leaned back on the chaise longue, her long face eloquently reflecting the despair she felt. But she didn't cry out or say anything, and made no effort to defend her husband. It was as if she had known all along, and had been waiting for this shoe to drop. Now it had, with a vengeance.

Skip waited a moment, finished his drink and stood up.

"Would you mind if I looked in your garage?" he asked gently.

She peered up at him through narrowed eyes. He thought he saw tears in them. "It's not in there," she said.

"Then it won't hurt for me to look."

"Do as you wish, Mr. Tracewski."

Skip clapped his hat on and shrugged into his coat. He felt lousy when he considered what the woman must be going through at that moment, and wanted to advise her to be careful, that her husband Frank was a very dangerous man when crossed. But then he figured she already knew that, judging from the size of the welt on her chin. He turned and left her on the chaise longue.

He checked out the garage, found only Carlotta's car, got into his Mazda and drove off.

CHAPTER 9

THE TOWN OF CARLTON BOASTED A TIMBERLINE TAVERN and a single Chevron gas pump in front of an unpainted grocery. Beyond that the highway continued over a narrow bridge. Skip drove across the bridge and slowed as he passed a liquor store, an abandoned church, and a one-room schoolhouse, also abandoned. Next to the schoolhouse, a yellow two-story frame house had been taken over by the United States Postal Service. A U.S. flag hung from a mast nailed to one of its porch posts.

Skip pulled into its small, unpaved parking lot, got out of the car and entered the post office. A tiny woman was standing on a wooden stool with a pack of letters in one hand, flipping them expertly into the sorting boxes with the other. As Skip stopped in front of the window, she glanced over at him.

"Hello, there," he said, removing his hat.

She stepped off the stool, put the letters down on her desk and approached the window. She was in her late fifties, wearing a purple dress with white lace at the throat. Her hair was blued; there was a dimple in her chin, and her hazel eyes loomed at him from behind Coke-bottle glasses.

"Yes?"

"I'm looking for an old friend."

"What're you sellin'?"

"Selling?"

"Ain't you a salesman?"

He laughed and shook his head.

"You needn't laugh," she said. "They're a real nuisance, I can tell you. They come by here with their little cards, lookin' for the people whose names are on them, and everyone complains you can't get rid of them. Like gnats in the evening. So I ain't supposed to tell on them—I mean, where they live."

"I sure wouldn't want to be pestered by a swarm of salesmen, either," Skip agreed. "The thing is, ma'am, I'm only just passing through, and when I saw I was comin' up on Carlton, I decided to surprise an old friend of mine. He's always nagging me to visit him up in these beautiful mountains you got. His name's Randall, Howard Randall. He's a big fellow. You couldn't miss him."

"Is he new hereabouts?"

"You mean is he a native?"

"Yes."

"Oh, no. Not Howie."

"Where does he work?"

"In Lake Placid. At a restaurant."

"Oh, *that* one."

"You know him?"

"I know *of* him. He's sure a strange duck. There ain't been a single letter for him since he took over the Farley Place."

"Where's that?"

"On Barrel Hill Road."

"He lives there, does he?"

"Yep. Some friend you got. He works as a bouncer at Violi's restaurant in Lake Placid."

"Yeah, that would be Howie, all right. How do I get to his place?"

"Keep on going. It's about ten miles out of town. Barrel Hill Road's about four miles past the Whitson farm on your right."

"The Whitson farm?"

"You can't miss it. They've painted everything fire-engine red. City folks. They just bought the place."

"Much obliged."

"You sure you ain't a salesman?"

"Positive."

She nodded. "Well, that Randall's got a dog, I heard. Doberman. Mr. Randall may be your friend, like you say. But you better be careful all the same."

She returned to her desk, took up the letters she was sorting and stepped back up onto her stool. He thanked her, left the post office and drove on out of

Bill Knott

Carlton. There were five more frame houses in the town of Carlton, and three of them had For Sale signs nailed to a tree or on stakes stuck in the front lawn. Not one was a Century 21.

He had no difficulty spotting the Whitson place. It came in sight about a mile after he passed a series of grim-looking farmhouses standing amidst collapsed barns and decapitated silos. After such a lineup, the Whitson farm stood out like a rose bush in a manure pile. Perched on a slight rise, the two-story frame house had four white columns in front, in dramatic contrast to its red clapboard siding. The huge red barn in back had a bright white trim. Maple trees shaded the house, and a gleaming whitewashed fence enclosed the rolling pastures and the Whitson's three high-stepping Arabians he glimpsed tossing their manes beyond the barn.

City folks for sure. Came out here for the fresh air and the good life. Which meant that about now they must be getting pretty damn lonely.

As he passed the Whitson place, a school bus loomed on a curve just ahead of him, its red lights flashing, reminding him that despite the summer weather, it was past Labor Day already. He pulled to a halt behind the bus and saw a little boy in a white shirt and tie hop down and run up the drive to a rambling, unpainted farmhouse. He was carrying a brand-new briefcase, one tailored to his size. He could not have been more than five or six, and his eagerness—or was it relief?—to get out of the bus and back home again was joyously apparent.

Skip couldn't help it. He was thinking now of his

own boy. Georgie had been no bigger than this lad when he started school, and Skip had purchased him a similar briefcase, with a pencil case inside that snapped open to the smell of crayons and newly-sharpened pencils. And like this little fellow, Georgie had been just as eager to get off the bus, his face as bright as a new penny as he burst into the kitchen to relate his day's accomplishments. Skip hadn't been home too often at such times, but when he was, he relished them. One of his deepest regrets was that he had not been in the kitchen more often when his boy came home.

As Skip watched, a screen door on the farmhouse's attached porch swung out and a plump, dark-haired woman in an apron held it open for the boy as he ducked inside.

The bus pulled forward, the lights snapping off, the driver keeping well off to the side to let Skip pass. He speeded up and swept past the bus, the painful tightness in his throat only gradually easing.

About four miles farther on he came to Barrel Hill Road, slowed and turned onto it. The road was unpaved, its ruts baked to a cementlike consistency. There had once been a sign post, but all that remained was a rusted relic, bent nearly flat to the ground.

He followed the ruts and after a quarter of a mile drove onto a narrow gravel causeway that sliced through an extensive swampland. Pussy willows and cattails lined both sides of the road's narrow shoulder, and farther out, the bleached skeletons of ash and maples poked up through the scummy water. He halted and, leaning out the window, listened to the vast, echoing chorus of frogs and cicadas. He liked the sound. He took his foot off the brake and kept on, putting the swamp behind him, soon catching sight of Moon's place ahead of him on the right.

He drove past it, turned cautiously on the narrow road, then drove back. Before he reached Moon's driveway, he nudged the Mazda off the road into a nearly impenetrable screen of lilac bushes. He got out of the car, took the ax from the trunk and pushed through the brush toward the house, coming out onto the driveway in front of it.

Moon's place was an unfinished sprawl of a house built on a slight rise. At the foot of the driveway was a huge weathered ruin of a barn, and in a field beyond it stood a toolshed and the remains of an old henhouse, its shingled roof barely visible above the weeds. Moon's Trans Am was not in the driveway. But a gray Ford Taurus was.

Despite the parked Taurus, the house had the feel of a place that, at least for now, was unoccupied.

Skip crossed the driveway, studying the ground in hopes of finding a trace of the Lamborghini's tire treads; they would be wider and flatter than those used on the usual Detroit or Japanese car. But he found no such tracks, and kept on toward what appeared to be a dismal caricature of what he supposed had once been someone's idea of a dream house. It was a single-story ranch style with a newly-shingled roof, employing the cheapest of red asbestos shingling. The windows were new Andersons, but their frames remained unpainted, and one

BODY PARTS

quarter of the front of the house was finished off with redwood siding, while the remainder was covered with tarpaper secured with odd pieces of lumber nailed across it. An unpainted deck ran the length of the house, the front door opening off it.

He mounted the deck's steps and peered in through the windows, looking for the Doberman. He saw no sign of the dog and was beginning to think it was a fiction beloved of the townspeople when he paused by the door with his hand on the knob, peered through its oval window and found himself gazing into the Doberman's satanic, unblinking eyes.

He tapped on the window. At once the dog leaped at the door in a snarling frenzy to get at him. It twisted in midair, leaping again and again. At last Skip tired of the game and left the door and moved on down the deck, peering through each of the windows as he passed, able now to see the Doberman keeping pace with him, padding alertly along just under the windowsills. He realized that the dog must have been there all along, keeping so close under the windows that he had been unable to see it. At the last window he tapped again on the glass, much louder than before. The Doberman leaped at the window, its lips curled back over its fangs, eyes glowing with pure malevolence. Skip involuntarily tightened his grip on the ax and felt his skin prickle at being this close to an animal so insanely eager to close its fangs about his throat. It occurred to him then that if he goaded the dog any further, its mounting frenzy to get at him might just enable the dog to hurl itself through the glass.

Bill Knott

Skip descended the deck's steps, crossed the yard and walked into the barn. Part of the back wall had fallen away, leaving a hole large enough to drive a car through. He glanced up. The loft's flooring did not look very solid. A few of the planks had rotted through, and tufts of moldy hay struck down through the cracks. Rolls of chicken wire, pitchforks, shovels, and milk cans lined the side walls, all of them covered with decades of grime and cobwebs. A six-cylinder engine block, its pistons removed, hung from a chain looped over what appeared to be the barn's only solid beam.

Skip walked farther into the barn, lifted a loose floorboard and slid the ax under it. As he straightened he heard a car coming down the road. He stepped out through the hole in the barn and pushed through the tall grass to the shed, ducked behind it and lowered himself into what he sincerely hoped was not a patch of poison ivy.

The Trans Am, with Moon driving and Luigi in the front seat beside him, swung into the driveway and halted. Moon remained behind the wheel as Luigi got out and walked over to the Taurus. Before he pulled open the door, Luigi turned and said something to Moon. The Neanderthal nodded, gunned his motor and swung the Trans Am around. Flooring the accelerator, he roared out of the yard.

Keeping his head down, Skip cut behind the shed and made for his own car. In his haste he crashed through a tangle of raspberry bushes and lost his hat. He swept it up, kept going and nearly tripped over a partially downed barbed-wire fence. A barb

BODY PARTS

sank into his pants leg. He yanked the pants free and plunged on. When he reached his car, he heard the Taurus turning out of Moon's driveway. He peered through the lilac bush and saw it heading down the road toward the highway. Skip backed his car out onto the road, waited until the Taurus was out of sight, then gunned the Mazda after it.

When Skip reached the highway, he glimpsed Luigi's Taurus heading north and swung out after it. When he came up on the Taurus, he hung back enough to allow a pickup truck to cut in between them. He kept the Taurus in sight as they climbed higher into the mountains, but after negotiating a long sweeping curve, he found only the pickup still in front of him.

He braked, drifted onto the soft shoulder to let a semi thunder past, then made a U-turn and drove back until he sighted a weed-choked logging road on his right. He kept on past it, pulled well off the highway, parked, then walked back to the road. A carpet of sun-bleached grass and pine needles prevented any tire treads crossing over them from showing. Bending to examine the grass between the ruts, however, he found a few strands still shiny black from transmission oil.

He set off on foot down the logging road.

This had sure as hell been a long day, he reminded himself wearily as he glanced down at his scuffed shoes. There was a tear in his pants leg where the barb had caught it. He kept on doggedly, and when the logging road ended at the edge of a clear-cut area, his coat was slung over his arm and he was using his hat to cool himself, his bald pate shiny with perspiration.

As he gazed across the clear-cut area, he was dismayed at the desolation the loggers had left behind. Not a tree was left standing, and very few bushes or saplings were struggling to emerge from the tangle of slash that covered the ground. He decided to skirt the clearing, since there was no way he could cross it in the open without exposing himself. He headed for a stand of young pine bordering a low ridge and plunged into it. Keeping in the pines, he followed the ridge as it circled the clearing.

He was onto the Lamborghini almost before he was aware of it. Pulling up, he glimpsed its white body gleaming just ahead of him beyond a thin screen of trees. As he watched, a pine branch thudded down onto its roof. A moment later another branch followed. Then another. Skip shifted his position to get a clearer view and saw Luigi, standing on the ridge just above the Lamborghini, tossing the branches down onto the car. He was working so hard he had loosened his tie and taken off his coat and vest. His motive was clear enough. He was covering the Lamborghini over completely to make sure it stayed hidden. He—and that included Frank Santorini—had no intention of delivering it tonight.

They had other plans, it seemed.

Skip stepped back and made a wide circuit, left the pines, and came out behind Luigi's Taurus. Keeping it between him and Luigi, he moved closer, the pine needles effectively muffling his footsteps. So intent was Luigi on covering the Lamborghini, he did

BODY PARTS

not hear Skip until he rounded the Taurus and approached to within ten feet of him.

Luigi whirled.

"Hello, there, Luigi," Skip said, pleasantly enough. "Need any help?"

"Hey, what the hell!"

Skip smiled and halted. Luigi took a step back.

"Jesus, mister," he said. "You got a habit of turning up at the craziest times."

Skip glanced past Luigi at the Lamborghini. "Looks like Frank has no intention of dealin' this car for them four kilos. Can't really say I'm surprised."

"Hell, man, stashing this beauty away is my idea. But I ain't worrying none. You're right. Frank ain't got no intention of dealing for that coke. And neither have you. You're hanging on to them four keys. Am I right?"

"Something like that. What about you, Luigi? You want to deal?"

"With you? Leave Frank out of it?"

"Sure, why not?"

Luigi relaxed some. "What've you got in mind?"

"You let me drive off with the Lamborghini and you can have the four kilos."

Luigi's eyes narrowed. "I better think about it. I don't know if it would be such a good idea for me to go against Frank. I mean right out in the open like that."

"What the hell, Luigi," Skip prodded. "Make your move. Now. Here's the car in front of me. You have it and I have the nose candy. I disappear, the Lamborghini disappears. You lay low with the four kilos and keep your mouth shut until the dust clears, then move out with no one the wiser. After all, why cut Frank in if you don't have to?"

"I'd trust Frank before I'd trust you, repo man. You're a civilian, for Christ sake. Besides, you wouldn't be stupid enough to bring them kilos out here with you."

"You sure of that, are you?"

"Sure enough."

"Hey, Luigi, be cool. You don't *have* to trust me. I'm not asking you to. See for yourself. The four keys are still in that blue suitcase you saw me take from Mary Lou's place. And right now it's sitting on the backseat of my car. You get the suitcase, I get the Lamborghini."

Luigi hesitated for only a moment. "Where's your car?"

"Just off the highway, near the entrance to the logging road. We could drive there in your car."

Luigi studied Skip's face for a moment, then glanced back at the Lamborghini, its roof thatched with pine branches. He took a deep breath and looked back at Skip.

"Okay," he said. "I'll drive us out there, see for myself like you said. But I aint' promisin' nothin'."

Luigi walked over to the spot on the ground where he had left his neatly folded coat and vest, put them on, brushed off his sharply creased pants, then walked with Skip to the Taurus. Skip got in the passenger's seat as Luigi got behind the wheel. The tires spun on the pine needles as Luigi gunned the engine and swept the car around, then drove across the slash-covered flat.

"Tell me something," Skip said when they had reached the loggers' road. "Were you with Moon when he started using that ax last night?"

"Yeah, I was there."

"You saw the whole thing?"

"I said I was there, didn't I?"

"Then why didn't you stop that Neanderthal?"

"You ever try to stop the wind? Once that geek got through the door, he was unstoppable. I never saw a man enjoys his work so much. Besides, why the fuck should I bother? That kid he whacked was nothin', just a horny punk."

Skip asked no more questions.

When they reached the highway, Skip directed Luigi to the right. When Luigi came to Skip's car, he pulled onto the soft shoulder just in front of it. Skip got out and walked with Luigi back to his car. Standing beside the rear door, Skip pointed in at Mary Lou's blue overnight suitcase resting on the backseat.

"I'll be goddamned," Luigi said, peering in at it through the window. "Just like you said."

He yanked open the rear door and reached in. As his right hand closed about the suitcase's handle, Skip rammed the door shut, catching Luigi between it and the car's frame. Straining, his face dark with the effort, Luigi managed to turn himself about so that his shoulders were solidly planted between the car and the door. He grabbed the door with both hands and slowly forced it back. The car's frame gave Luigi better leverage than Skip, whose perspiring palms began to slip on the door's slick finish. Luigi heaved. The gravel under Skip's feet gave way and he was forced to give ground. Immediately, Luigi flung himself out from behind the door and hurled himself at Skip.

There was a brief, close-in struggle, a lot of grunting and missed punches, until Luigi caught Skip on the side of his head, rocking him back. Skip felt his hat go flying. Head down, he slammed his shoulder into Luigi, drove him back against the car, then buried his fist deep into the kid's midsection. Luigi took the punch, gasping, but hung in there. He was a lot tougher than Skip had figured. Luigi twisted away, danced aside and reached into his back pocket.

A switchblade clicked open in his right fist.

Skip stepped back. Moving the blade slowly back and forth in front of him, Luigi advanced on Skip, his liquid eyes gleaming.

"You sonofabitch," he panted. "Oh, you smooth-talkin' bastard—coming at me like that. I'm goin' to cut you into sausage."

"You're all talk, punk," Skip told him, slipping out of his coat and wrapping it around his left arm.

A car whipped past without slowing. Neither man paid any attention. Luigi charged, slashing at Skip. Skip ducked aside, then rushed Luigi, parrying the knife with his overcoat. Luigi slashed at Skip again. A second time Skip parried the blade. The blade sliced into the coat, its tip catching in the material. Skip flung the coat aside, ripping the knife from Luigi's grasp.

BODY PARTS

Luigi hesitated.

Skip charged and caught his forehead with the flat of his hand, slamming Luigi's head against the car's solid frame, the back of it crunching against the thin metal gutter along the roof's edge. The blow was powerful enough to radiate up Skip's arm clear to his shoulder. Luigi looked at Skip with wide, dazed eyes. For a single murderous moment Skip hoped ferverently that he had cracked Luigi's skull, that he had killed him. He stepped back. Luigi's knees sagged as he sprawled forward. He landed facedown, his nose plowing up a patch of gravel.

Trembling from the exertion, his breath coming in short, painful gasps, Skip steadied himself and nudged Luigi's shoulder with the toe of his shoe. When there was no response, he kicked Luigi over onto his back and leaned closer to him. Luigi was not dead; his breathing was normal. But he was out cold.

Skip walked to his overcoat and picked it up. Luigi's knife clattered to the ground. He reached down, snapped the blade back into the handle and flung it into the brush. He put his coat back on and picked up his hat. A tractor trailer rocked past, spraying gravel and dust over both of them. Squinting his eyes to keep out the grit, Skip grabbed Luigi under his armpits, dragged him back to the Taurus and lifted him into the front seat. He shoved him all the way across it, then slid in behind the wheel and slammed the door shut. The keys were in the ignition. He started the car, made a U-turn, and drove back onto the logging road.

Bill Knott

He drove slowly, looking off the road for a good spot, and found it soon enough, a narrow aisle through a patch of young pines. He drove deep into the pines, until he was sure the car could not be seen from the road. He parked, then pulled Luigi off the car seat and dragged him to the rear of the car. He opened the trunk and dumped Luigi into it. Luigi groaned slightly when he hit the floor of the trunk, but he remained unconscious. Skip searched Luigi's pockets until he found the keys to the Lamborghini. Then he dropped Luigi's keys beside him and slammed the lid shut.

He walked back out to his Mazda. Mary Lou's overnight bag had landed on the floor behind the front seat. He reached in and poked it farther in under the front seat, then drove back onto the logging road and followed it until he came to within walking distance to the Lamborghini. He parked and walked over to the hollow into which the car had been driven. Slipping down into it, he found the Lamborghini to be in pretty good shape. Its rear wheels, however, were sinking into the damp ground. He cleared the pine branches off the car, swung up the door, climbed in and started the motor. It came to life with a healthy roar. He shifted into reverse, then forward, rocking the car gently, his foot barely caressing the accelerator. But he made little headway. The slick pine needles prevented the rear wheels from gaining any purchase, and soon the spinning wheels had dug themselves still deeper into the soft ground. Twice Skip got out of the car to place branches and twigs under the tires, but they were of little help as the tires sank even deeper.

He would need a wrecker, Skip decided.

He locked the Lamborghini, climbed out of the hollow and walked back to his car.

Skip unlocked the door to his room and pushed into it. Slumping on the bed, he reached for the phone and dialed Buford.

"I got the Lamborghini," Skip told him. "It's clean."

"Jesus, Skip. Nice going."

"I'll need a wrecker. You got the name of anyone up here who's worked with us before?"

"Yeah, there's two or three. The closest is in Saranac Lake."

"One will do."

"Wait a minute."

Skip closed his eyes and waited.

"Yeah, here it is," Buford said, coming back on. "You got a pencil?"

"Just give me his name. I can look it up."

"His name's Mel Dannenhower. Maple Street Mobil, Saranac Lake."

"Okay, thanks."

"You want me to run up there and give you a hand?"

"Why?"

"You don't sound so hot."

"It's been a long day, Buford."

"Okay, Skip."

Skip hung up, dialed information and asked for the number of the Maple Street Mobil in Saranac Lake. He took the number down in his notebook, hung up, and lay back full length on the bed. He was glad he had been able to deal with Luigi as he had. For a bad moment there he had wanted to kill the punk, and that would sure as hell have complicated things. Luigi would be pretty damn uncomfortable locked in that trunk, and he had probably already soiled his expensive suit and silk briefs; but he wouldn't suffocate and was out of it now, one less problem Skip had to worry about.

He took a deep breath and stared up at the ceiling.

Passing the Mirror Lake Lodge on the way into town, he had slowed and glanced to his left at the cottage on the lake shore where he and Louise had spent their honeymoon; it was like he had a bad tooth and couldn't keep his tongue from exploring it.

And he was still thinking of his boy.

Three days after his thirtieth birthday he had come home late to an ominously empty house. Louise had packed up and left him, and she had taken their seven-year-old son with her. She had left the house immaculate, the beds made with such military precision he could have bounced a quarter off the bed-spread—a calculated swipe at him he had realized at once through the swelling rage and bitterness that built within him as he stalked through the empty house, pausing only to make frantic, useless phone calls.

Though he pulled every string he could to find her

BODY PARTS

—including calling on the FBI—she had vanished as completely as if she and his son had left the planet. Three months later he had been asleep fully clothed on his couch when a call came a little after midnight from a sympathetic highway patrolman in Texas, telling him enough to freeze the blood in his veins, but keeping enough back so that when he flew in the next day he had been in reasonable control.

The highway patrolman, Frank Diaz, a swarthy man with dark, sympathetic eyes, met him at the airport and told him what he had deliberately kept from him—that his wife and son had not survived the crash. On their way to the morgue he told Skip that there had been three passengers in his wife's red 1981 Chevrolet Caprice when it wrapped itself around a bridge abutment, and that she had not been driving. The driver had been a Robert Dunhill, who had been speeding in excess of eighty miles an hour when he met the abutment. The autopsy revealed that his blood alcohol count had been high enough to have rendered him unconscious before he totaled the Caprice.

"You knew Dunhill?" Diaz asked.

"He worked at a real estate agency with my wife."

Diaz nodded and looked away, as if it were the oldest story in the world. Which it was.

Only after he had gazed down at Louise and seen how cruelly the windshield had sawed and ripped at her head and face, did Diaz lead him toward the small figure huddled under the sheet on the next slab. Nearing it, Skip pulled back. Diaz nudged him forward gently as the morgue attendant lifted the sheet.

A moment later he was able to give Diaz a positive ID for the third body. Skip had known Dunhill as a tall, handsome man with dirty fingernails, yellowing teeth, and blond wavy hair he sprayed heavily. A smooth, fast-talking hotshot, he had been the agency's award-winning performer until he was forced to resign for embezzling the agency's funds six months before Louise ran off with him.

He didn't look like much of a hotshot now.

"That's him," Skip muttered.

When he got back from Texas, he removed from his closet what few clothes he needed, left the house, and put it on the market. There was no way he could ever again live in his house, certainly no way that he could go into Georgie's room. And everything else in that house was a lie.

It would be impossible to make Terry understand why he refused to opt a second time for marriage and all that such a commitment implied—when a woman could drive off in a snit with some loser and take it all away from you.

He got off the bed and went over to the window, watching the people passing in the street and those in the boats on the lake beyond. Young men and women, pairing off as they were meant to do. Making plans, dreaming. Did they have any idea what lay ahead for so many of them? He chuckled suddenly, his spirits lifting unexpectedly. Hell, even if they did know, it wouldn't stop them.

And maybe it shouldn't stop him, either.

The phone rang.

He walked back to the bed, sat down on it and picked up the receiver, thinking it might be Buford calling him back.

"Yeah?"

"I'm right downstairs in the lobby," Terry told him. "I was going to surprise you, but the desk clerk won't let me. Can I come up?"

"What the hell're you doin' here, Terry?"

"That's a fine greeting, I must say."

"Hey, I'm just surprised, that's all."

"Remember? I told you what a lovely place Lake Placid would be for us to relax. And that's what I was thinking just now when you bit my head off."

"You should have given me some kind of warning."

"You mean you're not alone up there?"

"Only a couple of floozies. Just ignore them."

"Third floor, right?"

"Room 340. I'll leave the door open."

"I'll be right up."

"Terry?"

"Yes?"

"It's a motel, you know."

"Shut up," she said, and hung up.

CHAPTER 10

CAESAR LEANED HIS HEAD AGAINST THE APARTMENT door and listened. He heard nothing. Like Frank told him, the lock had already been forced, so he nudged the door open, pulled the .22 automatic out of his jacket's side pocket and moved silently down the hallway. He came to the bedroom and stepped into it. Son of a bitch. Empty. He dropped the .22 back into his pocket.

Frank told Caesar he had left the girl strapped securely to the bed and the nigger hanging from a nail. Caesar was supposed to make sure the nigger was dead, then O.D. the girl with the needle full of pure horse he'd given him. He was supposed to make it look like the nigger hung himself in grief because his white *puta* was dead. Caesar looked around the room. The ax Frank said he had left there to tie these two in with that motel shit was gone, too.

He didn't like it that Frank could be this wrong.

He left the bedroom and walked into the kitchen. The stench of rotting garbage came from a torn plastic bag under the sink. Bits of pizza crusts were ground into the linoleum. The sink was choked with food-encrusted dishes, and yellow Styrofoam hamburger cartons and pizza boxes littered the counters. He left the kitchen to check out the living room and found an untidy pile of books in one corner, old socks on the floor, and soiled briefs discarded along one wall. A torn, filthy rug covered the floor. The sofa's stuffing was hanging out. The smell in here was bad, too. It stank of an unclean human. And there was another smell. Turpentine.

He'd need a hose to flush out this place.

But it *could* be cleaned out, and living up here in this town, he would be away from all that Albany shit. Maybe up here he could find himself a blond chick to move in with him and keep the place tidy—if she wasn't a slob like so many of these *infama* American women.

He'd just go ahead and move in. He wouldn't bother with the landlord until he came around looking for the nigger. Then Caesar would tell him he didn't know nothin' about him. If the landlord tried to give him any trouble, he'd make the capitalist son of a bitch realize it was better to let him stay. Caesar smiled. This way he wouldn't have to bother with them goddamn credit checks.

But right now he'd better get back to Frank and tell him there was no dead nigger hanging from the wall like he said, and no blond *puta*. When he left the apartment, he jammed the door shut with a piece of cardboard torn from a pizza box. He'd have to fix that lock before he moved in.

Frank was sitting out on the deck, thinking how he was going to make it up to Horse Face. He'd have to, no question. His anger had vanished almost as soon as he got behind the Jag's wheel, and he realized that now was no time for him to start slapping her around. If this killing of Moon's blew up in his face, he might be needing her after all.

Good lawyers came expensive.

He heard someone open the door leading into the apartment and got to his feet. Through the glass doors he saw Caesar step into the living room, his narrow buttonlike eyes peering cautiously around.

Frank slid back the glass door. "Out here."

Caesar stepped onto the deck. Frank closed the door behind him.

"Well?"

"You must be crazy, Frank."

"What do you mean?"

"I don' find nobody. No nigger. No *puta*."

Frank wanted to believe Caesar was joking, only this zip never made jokes. "What the hell do you mean? I told you. I left the girl strapped to the bed, and that nigger had a wire around his neck."

Caesar shrugged.

Frank closed his eyes. He did not believe this shit. It was coming down in buckets. He had watched Moon strap Mary Lou to the bed, then hang Ahmed up on that nail again. When they left, the spade had been gagging on the hanger like a man already dead.

He thought then of Tracewski strolling into Ahmed's apartment, presenting his business card.

"Caesar, what about Moon's ax I left there?"

"I didn' see no ax."

"Jesus," Frank muttered softly. "Tracewski!"

Frank walked over to the deck's railing, gazed across the lake and shook his head. That son of a bitch. He had really believed all the repo man wanted was that fucking Lamborghini.

"Who is this Tracewski?" Caesar asked.

"A repo man. He told me he wanted to trade Mary Lou's car for them four kilos he took from her place."

"And you make this deal with him?"

"Hell," Frank snorted. "I wasn't *really* gonna deal with him. Soon's I got my hands on that nose candy, he'd be history."

"Where is this man?"

"I don't know. You got to find him, Caesar."

"Hey, Frank, you crazy? How can I find him? I never seen this man."

Frank dug Skip's business card out of his pocket and handed it to Caesar. "Here's the fucker's business card. See that Indian inside the tire? Luigi says the repo man's car's got a decal on its side just like that."

Caesar studied the business card for a moment, then glanced up at Frank.

"Hey, Frank, where do I look for this car?"

"Drive around. I figure this bastard's still in town. Maybe you can spot it. Check the parking lots. Maybe he's in a gin mill or checked into a motel. He's got to park somewhere. Just look for that fucking Indian in the decal. I want this son of a bitch, Caesar."

"What's he driving?"

"I don't know. But Luigi might know—or Moon. Ask one of them."

"Where's Luigi?"

"Moon drove him out to his place to pick up his car. They should be back by now."

Caesar nodded. "So I'll ask Luigi. You say he knows this man?"

"Sure. He's seen him."

"Maybe he better go with me."

"Good idea. Take Luigi. But if you spot this repo bastard, get back to me first before you move on him. Luigi says he's got Mary Lou's nose candy in a small blue suitcase he took from her house. We got to get our hands on that suitcase before we stomp him."

"That won't be so easy."

"Listen, Caesar, did I say this was goin' to be easy? I know it ain't. This fucker smiles a lot, but he's a bomb thrower. I got to stop him before he wrecks everything."

"I'll go downstairs," Caesar said, "get Luigi." Caesar slid back the glass door, then paused. "Hey, Frank, that nigger's apartment, I think maybe I'd like to move in there."

"Move into that place? It's a dump, Caesar."

"I'll clean it up."

Frank shrugged impatiently. "Okay, Caesar, okay. Live where you like. I don't care. Just find this asshole for me."

Caesar stepped into the living room and left the apartment. The phone rang. Frank walked back inside and answered it.

"Frank . . . ?"

It was Carlotta.

"Hi, honey," he said quickly. "Listen, I was just goin' to call you. I'm sorry about that little misunderstanding we had this morning. You all right now?"

"No."

The ice in her voice told Frank that, as he had already suspected, he had gone too far that morning. He took a deep breath. "All right," he said, his voice as cold as hers. "If that's the way you want it. I just told you I was sorry. What do you want me to do, crawl on my belly all the way up to the house?"

"Even if you did, Frank, it wouldn't do any good—not now."

"Look, we'll settle this later. Right now, I got other things to worry about."

"Like Mary Lou Dobbs?"

Oh, shit. "Carlotta, what're you talkin' about?"

"I'm talking about that white Lamborghini you bought for her."

"Hey, who's been feedin' you all this crap?"

"A Mr. Tracewski. Perhaps you know him. He looks like Mr. Clean. He just left here. I know what he told me is true, Frank, so I don't want any more bullshit from you."

He was astonished. He'd never heard Carlotta use that expression before. "All right, Carlotta, no bullshit. But I don't want you going off half-cocked. I can explain it all—just give me the chance."

"You can explain it to Carmine when he gets here."

Frank felt his stomach tighten. "Carmine? The don?"

"Your godfather, yes. Carmine. He's on his way."

She hung up and Frank stood there, staring at the phone in his hand, his mind racing. That goddamn Tracewski! What in the hell was that mother doing to him?

Frank slammed the receiver down and ran down the stairs, hoping to overtake Caesar. He rushed through the restaurant, nodding absently to a few early diners who waved to him. Moon was in his usual corner booth in the lounge, wolfing down a platter heaped high with spaghetti and meat balls.

"Where's Caesar?" he asked Moon.

"He just left."

"With Luigi?"

"I don't know. He asked where Luigi was, then he left."

"Well, where the hell *is* Luigi?"

"Ah don' know, Frank." The big oaf was frowning

Bill Knott

in concentration as he wound a huge, dripping gob of spaghetti around his fork.

With one furious sweep of his hand Frank knocked the fork out of Moon's hand and sent the platter of spaghetti flying. Silverware and a glass of beer went with it as the platter thudded off the wall, leaving a fist-sized portion of spaghetti and part of a meat ball adhering to the wall.

"You just finished eating," Frank told Moon. "Let's go!"

Stunned and resentful, Moon slid out of the booth. Too embarrassed to meet the eyes of the astounded patrons, he kept his head down as he followed Frank out the door.

Carlotta was crossing the drive on her way to the garage when Frank caught sight of her. He figured she must have realized how furious her call had made him and was now anxious to make tracks before he caught up with her.

Heading straight for her, he tightened his grip on the Jag's steering wheel and floored the accelerator. Startled, she froze, not knowing which way to go; then, with a scream, she flung herself off the driveway onto the lawn, jumped up and tried to run off, but as Frank braked the Jag and burst from the car, Carlotta's heels caught in the turf and she spilled forward onto the grass.

Frank held up and glanced at Moon, who was just emerging from the Jag. "Go get her!" he told him.

BODY PARTS

"Aw, shit, Frank! What's the matter with you? That's Carlotta!"

"I know who the fuck she is, you dumb cracker. I said go get her!"

As Carlotta got to her feet, Moon hurried over and grabbed her about the waist. She turned on him furiously and tried to pull free. When she couldn't, she began to beat futilely on his massive chest. Moon caught her wrists and held them. Carlotta began to cry.

Ignoring her tears, Frank walked over to her. "All right, Carlotta. Where the hell you think you're going?"

"Away from you!"

"Get her inside, Moon," Frank said, looking quickly about him for sign of the gardener.

"How dare you!" Carlotta railed at Moon. "Take your hands off me!"

"Ah didn't mean to hurt you none, Miss Carlotta," Moon told her as he stepped back and released her wrists.

"Go inside, Carlotta," Frank told her.

She flung herself about and stalked angrily ahead of them back into the house. Once inside, Frank told Moon to wait in the living room. Then he escorted a grim Carlotta into their bedroom.

"All right now," he told her, closing the door. "Let's have it. What's this about Carmine coming up here?"

"He's coming to see you. Because of what you did to me this morning."

Frank knew better. There was no way that would

Bill Knott

bring Carmine this far, not with all that RICO shit he was dealing with now. It must be something else Carlotta had told him.

He stepped closer to her. "What'd you tell him?"

"That you punched me."

He pushed her none too gently backward onto the bed. She kept herself upright, the mattress bouncing under her. "Now, Carlotta, I don't want no more shit from you. What'd you tell Carmine?"

"What I just told you."

He slapped her as hard as he could.

"It's true," she cried, her hand flying up to her cheek as tears welled into her eyes. "Carmine told me at the wedding. He told me to call him if I needed him."

She was weeping now, her face twisting grotesquely, and seeing her now—as if for the first time—Frank wondered how in the hell he had ever allowed himself to make love to this bitch.

"Listen," he said, bending over her threateningly. "Carmine wouldn't be coming up here just because I slugged you. Hell, he's always takin' a poke at his old lady. What else did you tell him?"

She began to edge across the bed away from him. "I mentioned something about . . . illegal drugs."

"Jesus," Frank said, straightening. "You told him that?"

She watched him, terrified, then nodded.

"Who wised you up? That repo man?"

"You mean Mr. Tracewski?"

"That's who I mean."

"No, he didn't say anything about that. It's what I

heard. Gossip. That's what I thought it was. From my friends."

"Yeah. Your friends—and *my* customers."

"I knew it wasn't gossip when Mr. Tracewski told me about you and that girl—and that car you bought her. It got me so mad. That's why I called you. I shouldn't have done that. I should've let Carmine drive up here and surprise you."

"When did you call him?"

"After you . . . struck me. Carmine said for me not to tell you he was coming up. He said he wants to surprise you."

"I bet he does."

Frank stepped back. He had enough loot stashed away to convince Carmine he set it aside for him as his percentage. Now if Caesar could get his hands on that repo man, Frank would have four keys to sweeten the pot. Meanwhile, the don wouldn't get up here before seven at the earliest, which would give him enough time to get Carlotta out of his hair. She was crazy enough to go to the cops—her lawyer, anyway. She wasn't family, which meant there was no way he could convince her to keep her mouth shut.

"Moon!" he called. "Get in here."

Moon appeared in the bedroom doorway.

"Take Carlotta out to your place. Tie her up if you have to, but keep her there. I don't care how you do it, just keep her there. I don't want to see her around here again. You got that?"

"Take her to my place?"

"Whatsamatter? You hard of hearing?"

Moon started for Carlotta.

"And take her car," Frank said.

"Don't you dare touch me," Carlotta told Moon, pushing herself away from him until her back was firmly against the headboard.

"Go with him, Carlotta," Frank told her. "Moon won't give you no trouble, long as you do what he says."

"But . . . but this is kidnapping!"

"Look at it this way. You'll be out in the country for a while—takin' a vacation."

"What will you tell Carmine? He'll want to see me."

"No, he won't. It's me he's coming up here to see, not you."

"You *are* dealing in drugs, aren't you?" she snapped, seething. "You're a drug king! A mobster! A member of the mafia, like in that movie, *The Godfather!*"

He chuckled. "Hey, what's the matter with you, Carlotta? Ain't you heard what the governor says, there ain't no such thing as a mafia. Now go along with Moon."

Carlotta lost her fight then and made no effort to pull free of Moon's grasp as he took her arm, pulled her off the bed and led her from the room.

After Skip left his door ajar for Terry, he lay back down on the bed. He was asleep when she entered the room. Terry sat down in a chair beside the bed

BODY PARTS

and let him sleep until she saw how late it was getting. Then she reached over and nudged his shoulder gently.

He opened his eyes and blinked sleepily at her.

"It's almost five o'clock, Skip," she told him. "You going to sleep all night?"

He sat up. "How long have I been out?"

She glanced at her watch. "Close to an hour."

"Do I snore?"

"A little. It was kind of cute, actually."

He ran his hands over his bald pate and took a better look at her. She was not in her troopers' uniform, and that was a treat in itself. Her auburn hair, tied back with a large bow, was drawn smoothly across her temples, highlighting the shape of her skull. The bow was black to match the halter she was wearing, its neckline plunging dramatically. Her black and white polka-dot skirt flared just enough to reveal the clean lines of her long legs—a calculated choice, he knew, since she was well aware how much he enjoyed the sight of long-legged women in skirts.

She smiled, her eyes glowing seductively. Tiny, bright flecks swirled in their hazel depths. He looked away, finding her beauty at this moment almost intimidating, like looking directly into the sun.

She sat down beside him on the bed.

"You look like you've been through the wringer," she told him. "Your pants are a mess. And your shoes, Skip! Why, I'm ashamed of you. They're caked with mud."

He nodded ruefully and kicked them off.

Bill Knott

"Did you find the Lamborghini?"

"I found it."

She was a cop suddenly, her eyes alert. "Anything else?"

"You mean something you can tell Larry."

"Why not?"

"Forget Larry and turn on the TV," he said. "See if you can find any local news. I need a shower."

"All right. Do that and I'll see what I can do about your shoes."

"I'd appreciate it."

He peeled out of his clothes and headed for the bathroom. When he finished his shower and padded back out on wet feet, rubbing himself dry, Terry was sitting in the soft chair by the bed, her legs crossed, a generous portion of her thigh on display.

She had turned on the TV.

"I sent your pants downstairs to be mended, sponged, and pressed," she told him. "They should be back soon." She leaned back in the chair. "So I've been wondering. What shall we do until we get your pants back?"

Wrapping the bath towel around his broad, powerful midsection, he sat on the edge of the bed. He saw that she had managed to clean his shoes for him. They looked a lot better, even without a fresh coat of polish. He glanced at her. She was waiting for his answer.

"I want to watch the local news."

"There's no local news until five-thirty."

"That wouldn't give us nearly enough time, Terry."

She wrinkled her pert nose. "Guess it wouldn't, at that."

"Besides, I'm still exhausted."

"No need to explain."

"Just thought I would."

"Drop it, all right?"

They sat for a long while in silence. It was amazing how easy it was for her to get him feeling guilty. He kept his eyes on the television screen. At last the local news came on, showing shots of the aftermath of a two-car collision on the Northway south of Plattsburgh. After a commercial, the state police were interviewed rounding up some youthful pushers caught selling crack in the local high school. The camera caught the youngsters with their heads down being pushed into the paddy wagon. Another commercial came on, loudly. An idiot Ford dealer made a screaming pitch, acting like an ass as he flung away his shirt and walked out from behind a Ford in his boxer shorts.

Skip looked away.

The news came back on. As the anchorman gave the background, Skip watched a shot of the Lands End Motel in Hudson Creek, the camera approaching the motel unit where Jimmy Vasquez had been murdered. For just an instant the camera moved jerkily and the light man's TV beam illuminated only a small portion of the motel room, and Skip saw again the bloodstains on the walls, the bedspread, and the floor. The cameraman went in as far as the bathroom, then turned around to let his camera sweep the room's blood-splattered walls one more time.

Terry uncrossed her legs and leaned forward, frowning intently. "My God, Skip," she said softly.

"It wasn't pretty."

"And you had to identify the body?"

"That's what I did."

"Oh, Skip . . ."

Trooper Larry Carmody came on then, towering over Sergeant Booker's round-shouldered figure. The TV reporter thrust his mike into their faces and asked if they had any leads on the killer. Booker shook his head and moistened his lips, obviously intimidated by the microphone. But Carmody was not at all bashful.

"We do have some leads," he calmly told the reporter. "But of course I'm not in any position to say much more than that."

"Is it true the killer used an ax?"

"That's a safe assumption."

"Do you have the murder weapon?"

"Not as yet."

"Captain, do you expect an early break in this case?"

Carmody smiled patiently. "I can't say."

"Then you have no clues, none whatsoever?"

"I wouldn't say that. As I said, we have some leads. Remember, Bob, this investigation is only a few hours old. We'll have more to say later."

"Would you classify this as a simple robbery?"

Carmody paused, pursing his lips. "No, I don't think I would."

"Then it's a crime of passion?"

"Again, Bob, it's much too early to characterize this crime beyond saying what it is in fact—a very brutal murder." He stepped back then to leave the field to Booker.

Ignoring Booker, the reporter turned to face the camera for his summing up. Skip got up and turned off the TV.

"Very smooth," he said to Terry.

"Larry?"

"Yes."

"You see what I mean, Skip? He's no one's fool."

"And he's the new breed?"

"Wouldn't you hope so?"

"I don't know what I hope. It's nice he doesn't think it's just a simple robbery."

"Well, of course he doesn't. He's smarter than that."

"We can talk about Larry later. Okay? Right now I'm hungry. How'd you like some Italian food?"

"Is there a good Italian restaurant here?"

"Across the lake. You like fettuccine Alfredo? It's their specialty."

"Of course. But why go so soon? It's still early."

"I told you. I'm hungry."

"So am I," she said, standing up.

She removed her halter and tossed it over the back of the chair. He saw for sure she was not wearing a bra. What the hell. She didn't need one. Unsnapping her skirt, she stepped out of it and dropped it onto the seat of the chair. With her magnificent swimmer's figure standing naked before him, she

Bill Knott

reached behind her head and untied the black bow and with a quick, practiced flick of her head sent her thick chestnut curls cascading down onto her shoulders. She turned back the bedspread and slipped sinuously between the fresh sheets. Eyes glowing, she waited for him to join her.

He did so with an almost clumsy eagerness, wanting her suddenly with a ferocity that caused her to recoil momentarily—then join in with a quick, delighted laugh.

CHAPTER 11

Moon was two months into his sixteenth year when his mother called him into her bedroom on a sultry August night and told him she was feeling poorly and needed comfort. A single sweaty bedsheet was wound carelessly about her, scarcely covering her naked body. The pungent smell of Junior Perry's moonshine hung heavy over the bed, the jug on the floor beside it. As he stared down at his mother's freckled features, her long, bony face shiny with perspiration, she opened her arms to him and said she wanted a kiss.

Dutifully, he bent to kiss her cheek, but at the last

Bill Knott

moment she turned her head and her lips closed over his, opening eagerly, sending a sudden, electric quickening clear down to his crotch. Astonished and appalled, he tried to pull back, but her other arm, tight around his neck, held his mouth hard against hers. Reaching out hungrily, the fingers of her other hand closed about the growing bulk in his crotch and she pulled him down onto the bed beside her.

Her lips released his. "Are you Mom's big boy now?" she asked, her hot breath nearly smothering him.

"Mom, please. Don't!"

"Oh my, yes," she said, feverishly unbuckling his belt and reaching into his private parts. "You are! You're Mom's big boy. I can feel how big."

"Maw! You been at the jug. You don't know what you're doin'!"

"Hush now, Howie. Your mom needs a man."

He tried to push himself off the bed, but she kissed him again and did things with her tongue that shocked him profoundly—and melted any resolve to pull away he tried to muster; before he could stop her, she was stripping him of his pants.

"Cover me, oh, cover me," his mom cried, spreading her legs. "May the Lord Jesus forgive me, but I need you so bad!"

Clumsily at first, his big, strapping body pushed up onto her, while her feverish hand reached down to guide him, and when it was all over and he lay beside her, exhausted and bewildered, she held his face tight to her breasts and, sobbing with remorse,

BODY PARTS

vowed in the name of Jesus never to do such a wicked thing again.

But it was a vow neither of them could keep.

For Moon, during the two years that followed, his initial horrified reluctance was replaced by a raging need, easily as ferocious as hers. All his mother had to do was rest her hand on his forehead or brush against him and he was as eager to join her in bed as she was to have him.

Only now she began treating him not like her son, but her husband, nagging at him, flying at him for the slightest thing, never letting him be. He couldn't even go fishing without her coming after him. It was like she was so ashamed of their monstrous wickedness that she had to take it out on him. And they never once left the ridge together. It was like they knew anyone who saw them together would know at once how they spent their nights.

So he was the one she sent to Sonny Bigger's general store in the valley to spend their welfare check the first of each month. To those sitting about the potbellied stove who inquired of his mother's health, he replied only that she was feeling poorly. The lines around their eyes told Moon they knew why she was feeling so bad. Junior Perry's moonshine. But young Howie Randall was too massive a young man for them to mess with, so they clucked sympathetically, nodded their heads, and made no comment.

They did not know that for close on to two years his mother had sworn off Junior Perry's moonshine—and she kept to her vow, too, until the day he returned from Bigger's store to find his mother stinking

167

of moonshine, passed out on her bed. He had been furious, and once he sobered her up, she promised him tearfully she would never again soil her mouth with Junior Perry's moonshine. Later that night, with her watching in solemn penitence, he shattered the five more jugs of moonshine he had discovered hidden in the barn.

In the weeks that followed, she nagged at him relentlessly, never letting him rest, her tongue sharper and more disapproving than ever. The next month, instead of driving all the way to the valley store, he parked the pickup in a logging road a few miles down the road and walked back to the ridge. As he suspected, Junior Perry's truck was parked in their driveway. He stole to the bedroom window and through the torn lace curtains saw how his mother had purchased her moonshine the month before.

He ducked away from the window, the urgent squeak of the bedsprings tearing at his ears like claws, and ran for the woodshed. When he reached it, he was sobbing openly, a blind, murderous fury consuming him. He snatched up his ax and was still sobbing when he broke into the bedroom a moment later and decapitated the two lovers. He kept on hacking at them until bloody chunks of their mutilated torsos were scattered about the small bedroom.

Still clutching the ax, he ran all the way to his pickup, threw the bloody weapon into the bed of his truck and drove off. He was so blinded by tears, he had difficulty keeping on the narrow, rutted roads that took him out of the county. When he ran out of

BODY PARTS

gas, he abandoned the truck and hiked to a major highway and hitched a ride out of Kentucky, coming to ground at last in a small town near Atlanta.

That was seventeen years ago.

Now, watching Carlotta, Moon felt a sullen restlessness. The way Carlotta was carrying on, he found himself thinking of his mother and how she, too, had insulted him, finding fault with everything he did and ordering him around like he was her servant.

Earlier, when Carlotta stepped inside the house and caught sight of Devil trotting toward her for a pat, she had screamed, then demanded he lock the Doberman away in one of the bedrooms. He protested, told her the dog would not attack her unless she came at him. But she insisted, said she couldn't stand attack dogs, no matter how well they were trained.

Carlotta stood now in the middle of his living room, hands on her hips, sweeping the untidy room with a withering glance. Shaking her head bitterly, she slumped down into his rocking chair.

"This place is a pigsty, Moon," she told him scathingly. "Don't you ever pick anything up?"

He shrugged and looked around him. He agreed. The place was a mess. But so what? Who cared? This was the only room he used, so sure it was cluttered. It served as his bedroom as well as his living room. Aside from the kitchen, he saw no need for the other rooms.

"You live like an animal," she snapped, rocking angrily.

That rocker was his favorite chair and he missed it. He sat down on the edge of his bed.

"Miss Carlotta," he told her. "I wish you'd shut up. Ah don't care how this place looks to you."

"Insolent. You're insolent, too."

"I'm just doin' what Frank told me."

"You're his slave, is that it?"

"No, ma'am, ah surely am not."

She snorted derisively. "I think if Frank told you to walk off the end of the earth, you'd do it."

Moon moistened his lips unhappily. "Ah surely do wish you'd shut up, Miss Carlotta."

Ignoring his plea, she kept right on. "I want you to know I'm going to press charges. For kidnapping. You'll go to jail, and so will Frank when I get through with him."

Her voice was high and disturbing. He wanted to clap his hands over his ears to shut out the raw sound. If only she would shut her mouth. He didn't want to hurt her. Before this, she had always treated him with kindness, even consideration, like his mother had before she went back on Junior Perry's moonshine.

And she would *not* stop. She kept on and on and on . . .

". . . Oh, I know what you are now, Moon—a dumb Georgia cracker. That's what. All you're good for is to beat people with your fists and drive them from the lounge. What a lovely job."

He glowered at her but said nothing.

"A bouncer. That's all you're good for."

He did not reply.

"Did you hear me? I said that's all you're good for!"

"Shut up, Miss Carlotta," he said, his head lowering like a dumb beast that had been clubbed almost to insensibility.

"I won't!"

"If you don't, I'll have to make you."

"Are you threatening me?" she demanded.

"Yes," he told her helplessly.

She leapt out of the rocker, marched over to him and slapped him on the face with such force, involuntary tears stung his eyes. Before she could step back he grabbed her wrist and flung her down onto the bed. When she tried to pull free of his grasp, he punched her in the jaw. She screamed. He hit her again to shut her up. When it didn't work, he hit her once more, much harder.

The powerful blow silenced her at last. Barely conscious, she sprawled back on the bed, legs splayed. Aroused to a sudden, intense pitch, Moon unbuckled his belt, flung off his pants and knelt astride Carlotta's body. He flung up her skirt and ripped off her panties with one brutal tug, then thrust her thighs apart and, with an explosive grunt, plunged into her.

After combing three other motel parking lots, Caesar found Tracewski's car in the lot in front of the Thunderbird Motel. By that time he had searched two shopping mall lots, and while driving through the town, had even scanned the cars parked along the curbs.

He was pleased with his success in spotting the repo man's car. When he'd left Frank's place without Luigi, he wouldn't have given a cat's ass for his chances of finding it. But here it was. And he'd done it without Luigi's help. The decal on the door was a perfect copy of the one on the business card Frank had given him. Caesar stepped back to look more closely at the Mohawk Indian staring out at him from inside the tire. A mean-looking bastard.

He tried the car's doors. They were all locked. He glanced quickly around, then looked into the back-seat, shading the window with an upraised hand so he could see inside. He saw no blue suitcase on the back or the front seat, and wasn't surprised. No way this repo man would be leaving all that nose candy in his car outside the motel.

He remembered he was supposed to let Frank know when he found the car. But now that he knew where this monkey was, he would just as soon go in the motel and take out the bastard right now. But Frank was the boss. Caesar entered the Thunderbird lobby to look for a pay phone, and found one in a corner next to a Coke machine. He started to dial, then realized he didn't have the number to Frank's restaurant. When he found himself arguing with the information operator—the stupid cunt insisted there was no Frank's Italian Restaurant listed in the directory—he slammed the phone down and crossed the lobby to the front desk.

The desk clerk was a punk American kid in Levi's

BODY PARTS

and a sport shirt, no dress shirt and no tie, and his hair was as long as a girl's. Caesar stared at him with undisguised contempt as he waited for him to finish checking in a couple.

"Yes, sir," the desk clerk said when he had finished with the couple. "Can I help you?"

"Yeah. Maybe you can. A friend of mine's registered here. Name's Tracewski. What's his room number?"

"Mr. Tracewski?" He consulted his register. "That would be Room 340."

"Three forty, eh? Good. I think I go up now and give him nice surprise."

"He'd prefer you call first, sir. You can call from here." The clerk pushed the desk phone toward Caesar.

Caesar looked at the phone, then at the clerk. "Naw, I don' wanna call him. Like I said, I give him good surprise."

"Sorry," the clerk insisted. "Mr. Tracewski left word. He'd prefer you called before going up."

"Hey, whatsamatter, can't you hear good?" Caesar flared. "I already tol'a you. He's an old friend!"

The clerk pulled back at Caesar's sudden vehemence. Caesar spun angrily about and walked across the lobby to the elevator. He punched the up button, then glanced back at the front desk and saw the desk clerk talking urgently into the phone. The sonofabitch was calling Tracewski's room, warning the repo man that he was on the way up.

The elevator door slid open. Caesar moved aside to let the motel guests get off, then decided against

173

Bill Knott

using the elevator. That repo son of a bitch would be waiting for him now.

He hurried outside to his car.

Skip said into the phone, "Thanks," and hung up.

"Who was that?" Terry asked, coming out of the bathroom. She had just finished freshening herself up and looked great. On her cheeks there was still a trace of the glow Skip had helped put there.

"The desk clerk. He says we got a visitor on the way up."

The phone rang again.

Skip grabbed it. "Yeah?"

"That fellow isn't on the way up anymore, Mr. Tracewski," the desk clerk told him. "He saw me calling you and didn't get into the elevator."

"Where'd he go?"

"Outside."

"What's he look like?"

"Well, he's not very tall."

"Anything else?"

"I figure he's Italian—just off the boat, in fact. He has an accent."

"Thanks, kid. I owe you."

"No sweat, Mr. Tracewski."

Skip hung up and looked over at Terry. "I am afraid we're going to be disappointed. Our guest has decided not to show."

"Our guest? What's this all about, Skip?"

"You still up to that fettuccine?"

"Darling, after that glorious tumble, I'm famished."
"Me, too. I'll explain on the way."

———

As Skip drove the Mazda out of the motel parking lot, he glanced in the rearview mirror and saw a beat-up white 1980 Chevrolet Monte Carlo pull away from the curb and gun after him. As he had expected, he was going to have an escort all the way around the lake to Violi's restaurant.

"Now," Terry said. "Explain."

"About what?"

"That visitor, for one."

"He's working for the owner, or manager—I'm not sure which—of the restaurant we're patronizing tonight. A Mr. Frank Santorini. Frank's a mobster, and I imagine he's doing nicely supplying happy dust to this resort town's upper crust."

"What's all this got to do with Jimmy Vasquez's murder?"

"You mean what's it got to do with the Lamborghini."

"Have it your way."

"Frank Santorini has the car. But he's willing to deal."

"Whoa, Skip. You're going too fast for me. Didn't you tell me you already found the car?"

"The thing is, Santorini doesn't know that."

"What's this deal you mentioned?" Terry was non-stop questions.

"Four kilos of Peruvian flake for the car."

Bill Knott

"You mean you're going to give him the cocaine, even though you already have the car?"

"I want to make him. And you'll be the ideal witness when the poor sap tests the stuff and pays me for it."

"You're sure this'll stand up—that he won't be able to turn around and call it entrapment?"

"I'm sure."

"Maybe you can tell me how you knew I'd be coming up here tonight to be your witness?"

"I didn't. I had other plans, but now that you're here, I like this one better."

"Do you have the contraband with you?"

Skip nodded. "In an overnight bag on the floor under my seat."

"Where'd you get it, Skip?"

"That's my secret."

"Four kilos, you say. My God, that's a lot."

"Don't worry. All I've got with me is a small sample."

"Aren't you afraid that might cause trouble?"

"Not with you at my side, Wonder Woman."

"You're just saying that to be nice."

He glanced into the rearview mirror. The Monte Carlo was still hanging close. He had no doubt the driver was the short man with the Italian accent who didn't want to be announced. If he was just off the boat as the clerk suggested, he could be a zip, one of the Sicilian mafioso brought over to support the Pizza Connection. He was going to be very surprised when the Mazda turned down Greentree Road.

"Seriously, Skip," Terry said, "this could be dangerous."

"As long as neither of us is armed, and as long as we're dining in one of Lake Placid's most frequented night spots, I doubt if we'll be in any real danger."

She sighed. "I suppose you know what you're doing."

"Not entirely. I'm making this up as I go along. Which reminds me. You haven't mentioned Larry lately."

She leaned her head back against the seat and turned to look at him, her eyes lovely in the dark. "It has occurred to me that you do not like it when I mention his name. And making you unhappy, Skip, was not my reason for driving up here."

He reached over and patted her knee. "And so far, you've done very well."

"You were no slouch, either."

"So when we get to the restaurant, maybe you should give Larry a call. If you think you can reach him at this hour."

"I'm sure I can. But why should I?"

"He's looking for the murder weapon. Right?"

"Of course."

"I know where it is."

"Skip! The ax?"

"Tell him to meet us here at the restaurant."

"You devil."

He glanced at her, smiling. "See? This way there'll be no trouble at all. I'll be under the protection of not one, but *two* state troopers."

Skip cut down Greentree Road. Glancing into the

rearview mirror, he saw the Monte Carlo turning onto the road right behind him. That's the boy, zip. Join the party. The more the merrier.

Caesar couldn't believe it. This damn fool Tracewski was heading for Frank's restaurant. He kept close on his tail, following him right into the parking lot. When the repo man pulled to a halt, Caesar drove on past him, parked, and watched Tracewski and the woman get out of their car. The woman, he could not help noticing again, was a knockout. As he watched, she started for the restaurant's entrance.

Alone.

Immediately wary, Caesar got out of his car. Where the hell was Tracewski? He heard the gravel crunch behind him, turned and saw the son of a bitch approaching him. He was smiling and carrying a small blue suitcase. Aching to ventilate the bastard, Caesar pulled the .22 out of his side pocket and screwed on the silencer.

The trouble was, he hadn't contacted Frank yet.

"Put that toy away," Tracewski said, halting in front of him. "Frank wouldn't like that. We got a deal. Kill me, and you kill the deal." He lifted the blue suitcase and patted it affectionately. "I got the goodies right here."

Caesar lowered the .22.

"Now go in and tell Frank I'm ready to deal. It's a little earlier than I planned, but he'll understand."

The repo man turned his back on Caesar and

BODY PARTS

headed for the entrance to the restaurant. For just a crazy minute, Caesar considered cold-cocking the son of a bitch and dragging him up to Frank's apartment. But the creep looked too heavy for that. Caesar unscrewed the silencer and dropped the .22 back into his pocket, waited until Tracewski entered the restaurant, then hurried around back and mounted the steps leading to Frank's deck. Frank was relaxing in a lounge chair, a drink in his hand.

"You find him?" he asked when he saw Caesar.

"I found him."

"I told you to call me."

"He's downstairs in the restaurant. He has the stuff with him. He said he's ready to deal."

"I don't believe it," Frank said, getting to his feet. "That crazy bastard. Walkin' in here like that, after what he's been up to."

A heavy car crunched to a halt in the lot below the deck, the motor purring like a great cat. Frank peered over the deck's railing. It was a black limousine with New Jersey plates, and he did not have to be told who was sitting in the backseat.

"Get inside, Caesar," Frank said. "We got ourselves a visitor. Come all the way from Jersey."

CHAPTER 12

Skip entered the restaurant. Terry was using the phone on the wall next to the men's room to call Larry. He paused at the lounge entrance and looked in, expecting to catch sight of the Neanderthal. Moon was not in there. He was not needed yet. The evening was still young.

He kept on and paused at the entrance to the dining room, where a sign said, PLEASE WAIT TO BE SEATED. So he waited for the hostess to show up. When she appeared—a tall, gum-chewing blond with cartoon cleavage—he told her he was a special guest of Mr. Santorini's and would like a quiet booth in the back. He followed her well-oiled hips past candlelit tables to a booth in the rear close to the kitchen.

"My dinner guest is on the phone in the lobby," Skip told the hostess. "Would you please show her to this table when she finishes her call?"

"Sure," the girl said, still chewing.

She dropped two enormous glossy menus on the table and left him. A moment later Terry stopped behind the sign and waited. Still chewing, the hostess walked over to her and pointed in the direction of Skip's table. Skip was impressed. He couldn't wait for that fettuccine Alfredo.

Terry slid into the booth opposite him and took up the menu. "Larry will be here in a half hour—maybe sooner."

"Good. This'll probably make him."

"I know."

"Once you get the murder weapon, it's usually not too difficult to crack a case. And this one should keep the boys at BCI happy for a week."

"I could ask you how you found it, but you'll probably tell me you tripped over it while you were looking for the Lamborghini."

"How'd you guess?"

"Why are you doing this for Larry? I didn't think you liked him."

"There're others I like less. And besides, it's time that whiz kid got his nose out of those sociology texts and took a look at what's going on in the real world."

She leaned back suddenly. "I see. You're teaching Larry a lesson."

"I didn't mean it to sound like that."

"Well, that's just how it sounded. Honestly, Skip, sometimes I—"

"Don't say it, Terry," he warned.

She caught herself, glanced cursorily at the menu, then let it drop.

"We came here for the fettuccine Alfredo," she reminded him. "All right. That's what I'll order."

"Fine."

Skip put aside his menu. A waitress came over, filled their water glasses and took their order for drinks. When she left, Skip looked around. There was no sign of a band, and without it the bandstand looked abandoned, almost forlorn. The lighting was dim enough to conceal the fading paint and the cracks in the walls—and at the same time impart to the place a vaguely menacing ambience, one that obviously pleased the crowd that the young waitress had told Skip now frequented the place. Skip understood why the girl and her boyfriend no longer came here.

Their drinks arrived and Skip ordered for them both. When the waitress left, he glanced at Terry, but no longer found encouragement there. The idea of his teaching Captain Larry Carmody a lesson about the real world had not gone over very well. He sipped his Coors and glanced at the kitchen's swing doors, not five feet from their booth. They were thumping continuously. Terry followed his gaze as a waitress burst from the kitchen, carrying a full tray.

"This is a terrible spot," she said. "Couldn't we do any better?"

"I needed a booth where Santorini and I could talk in something close to privacy."

"Where's that suitcase?"

"Beside me on the seat," he said, reaching over to pat it.

"Really, Skip. This is all so theatrical."

"Life is theater."

"Now where did you hear that?"

"It just occurred to me."

"Sounds like something you read somewhere," she insisted.

Why was it, he wondered, that any time you said something interesting to a woman, she immediately assumed you read it somewhere? He said nothing in response, astonished as always at how quickly she could turn on him.

The waitress brought them hot rolls in a small wicker basket, and a moment later their soup du jour arrived. Beef and macaroni soup.

Skip found it delicious.

※

Carmine DiAngelo was a big man in the rackets and a big man besides. In fact, Carmine's girth was such that whenever he lowered himself into a chair, people averted their eyes; the sight of him struggling to get out of a soft sprung sofa was equally unsettling. At such times, despite the Florida tan, his porcine face would turn beet red. Though the ex-stripper he

BODY PARTS

stayed with tried to stop him from smoking, a cigar was always planted in his bulldog mouth. Someone at a table in a Little Italy restaurant remarked that the don reminded him of Tony Galento. The remark didn't get very far, since only the old-timers at the table knew who Galento was. Carmine heard about it, but made no trouble for the big mouth. The fact was, Carmine had liked Galento and didn't mind the comparison, even though he won a carload of green betting against the crazy heavyweight and his huge beer belly.

While Caesar had been tailing Skip to Frank's restaurant, Carmine DiAngelo was nearing Lake Placid in the back seat of the Lincoln limo he'd leased from the All America Leasing Corporation in Jersey City. The leasing company was owned by his wife's cousin, which meant, of course, that as a courtesy to the don, Carmine would not even have to consider paying a rental fee. It was not a stretch limo, but there was enough room in it for him to stretch out comfortably in the backseat. The ride had been a long one and he had taken no one with him, so he was bored, his teeth clenched impatiently on his cigar as he peered out at the desolate upstate countryside.

Gus had made good time, and they were already off the interstate, following a winding state highway into Lake Placid. Gus had been stopped only once on the Northway, and a century note had seen them past that annoyance. His snap brim pulled down over his forehead, Carmine had managed to keep his face completely hidden from the trooper. With his

Bill Knott

mug all over the Jersey City and New York papers this past couple of months, his face had become all too familiar—and the last thing he wanted was a frisk by some baby-faced trooper.

They entered Lake Placid. Leaning forward, Carmine tapped Gus on the shoulder, the effort causing him to wheeze slightly.

"Keep on this narrow main drag," he instructed Gus. "Follow it around the lake. Greentree Road's on your right."

"Is this lake we're driving past Lake Placid?"

"No, and I don't know where the fuck that lake is. This here lake is what they call Mirror Lake."

Gus nodded and eased smoothly through the heavy traffic, on past the shops and motels that crowded the two-lane thoroughfare, then cut right and kept on around the lake. As they approached Greentree Road, Carmine told Gus to watch out, they were coming up on it. Gus nodded and a moment later, smooth as silk, he turned down the road.

As they saw the restaurant ahead, Carmine told Gus not to park in front but to drive around and find a spot in the rear of the restaurant.

Gus nodded. The tires crunching over the gravel, he threaded through the banks of parked cars, turned the corner of the restaurant and brought the Lincoln to a smooth stop just under a deck jutting out from Frank's apartment on the second floor. Gus was out of the car in a second, opening the door for Carmine, his hand reaching in to help him, doing it so effortlessly and smoothly that Carmine expended hardly any effort at all. This unspoken consideration

BODY PARTS

on Gus's part was the reason Carmine would go nowhere without the bodyguard, and why Gus had been able to put so much money aside from his chauffeur's salary that he had already purchased a condo in Fort Lauderdale.

"Stay down here," Carmine told Gus. "Take a leak in the restaurant if you want, then come on back outside and wait in the car. I might need you. Frank's a horse's ass, and there's no telling what he's into. You got something to read?"

It was a foolish question. Gus *always* had something to read resting on the front seat beside him.

"Sure. Don't worry about me, Mr. DiAngelo. I'm all set."

Carmine left the car, grabbed hold of the wooden railing and used it to help him climb the steps. Heaving himself onto the deck finally, beads of sweat standing out on his forehead, he glanced through the glass doors and saw Frank in the living room with Caesar Amato. The sight of Caesar was unexpected and caused Carmine to chomp down angrily on his cigar. So now that crazy zip bastard was working for Frank.

Carmine pushed aside the sliding glass door and stepped heavily into the apartment.

"Hiya, Frank," he said. "How's it going?"

"Jesus, Carmine," Frank said, "you gave me a start coming in like that."

"How'd you expect me to come in?"

"Hey . . . no harm done, Carmine," Frank replied hastily. "How was the drive up from Jersey?"

Carmine saw at once that Frank had been expecting him. Which meant Carlotta had blabbed. Tell a dame not to let on, and she'll break through a brick wall to bugle it to the world. Standing there, Carmine felt Caesar's cold, raisin-black eyes on him, but he made no effort to acknowledge Caesar's presence. Nor did Caesar step forward to greet him, the sonofabitch. It occurred to Carmine that he should've kept in force that contract he'd offered for the bastard after what he done, but on Frank's plea he had called off the dogs. Caesar should've been grateful. But you could expect gratitude sooner from a mad dog than from a Sicilian.

Frank looked out the glass door past Carmine to see if anyone else might be standing on the deck.

"You come all this way alone, Carmine?"

"Gus is downstairs."

"Hey, Carmine. Gus is always welcome. He don't have to wait in that car. He can come up here for a drink, have something to eat."

"I know that, Frank. But he'll be okay down there."

"Have it your way, Carmine. Hell, make yourself at home. Sit down. Take a load off."

Frank was sorry he had used that term, and Carmine relished the dismay on Frank's face when he did. Carmine settled carefully at one end of the sofa, holding its arm.

"You got anything for me to drink, Frank? I ain't had a thing since two this afternoon."

"Hey, what's the matter with me! Sure thing. The usual?"

"I'm too old to change my habits now. No matter what the fucking doctor says."

Frank turned to Caesar. "Make Carmine a double vodka. On the rocks. You got all you need in the kitchen."

Caesar walked into the kitchen, and during the awkward silence that followed, they could hear the zip opening the cabinet over the sink, then the chink of bottles being pushed aside as he reached in for the vodka.

His voice low, Carmine muttered, "So now you got this Sicilian here working for you, huh? What the fuck do you need him for?"

"What can I say, Carmine? He didn't like Albany. He's already picked himself out a nice apartment across the lake. He likes it here. Happy as a pig in shit."

Carmine waved his fat bejeweled hand irritably. No sense in arguing with Frank about the zip. Not now, anyway.

"Where's Carlotta?"

"You don't need to see her, Carmine."

"Don't I?"

"She was way out of line calling you."

"Maybe so, Frank, but you ought to treat her better."

"Ah, you know women, Carmine. She gave me some lip."

"Was it right what she said—you foolin' with this quiff, buying a car for her?"

"Sure, I was foolin' around, Carmine. So what else is new? I mean this little lady had a helluva lot more talent in bed than Horse Face." He grinned at Carmine. "And she gave inspired head."

"Well, that's fine, Frank. I'm real happy for you. So what are you going to do about Carlotta?"

"Right now she's out at Moon's place, coolin' off."

"You mean you left her alone out there with that crazy redneck? Jesus, Frank."

"I had no choice, Carmine. She went apeshit. She was calling everybody. I figured the FBI was next. Don't worry about her. She'll be fine out there, no shit. Moon's a cracker, but he thinks anyone who has a lot of money and lives in a big house is better than he is. Besides, he respects her."

"How long do you think that'll last?"

Frank shrugged. "Let's talk about something else, huh, Carmine?"

"All right, so we forget Carlotta. Fuck her. She ain't my responsibility. Besides, that ain't why I'm up here."

"I know that, Carmine. I wasn't born yesterday. You think I been holding out on you."

"You tellin' me you ain't?"

"As a matter of fact I would've called you myself early next week. But I had a deal cooking and wanted to wait until I completed it. You beat me to the punch by only a couple of days. Stay right there. I got something to show you."

Frank opened a closet and lifted an aluminum attaché case off the shelf. Putting it down on the Formica table near the kitchen, he snapped it open and stepped back.

"Two hundred and sixty thousand bills," he

crowed. "Go ahead, Carmine. Count it. This here's your share of the operation. I've been saving it for you."

Carmine heaved himself out of the sofa and waddled heavily over to Frank. He took the cigar out of his mouth and leaned forward to peer more closely at the neatly folded bills. "You mean this is my split?"

"What else, Carmine?"

"Holy Christ, Frank. How come you're pullin' in so much up here?"

"Hey, Carmine, you thinkin' there's no scratch up here? Man, let me clue you in. This here's a famous resort. But it's an old resort. *Old* money, Carmine. That means plenty of it, with nothing to do but spend it. And the thing is, these airheads really believe in recreation. So that's what I'm pushing, Carmine. No crack, no horse. Recreational drugs: snoot dusters. Colombia flake. Hell, Carmine, these jerks take it in the morning with their steak and eggs and with their cocktails in the afternoon. And there ain't no price they ain't willin' to pay—within reason."

Carmine reached down and ran his fingers over the neat piles of bills. Old money. Easy to clean. He glanced at Frank.

"You were right, Frank. After what Carlotta said, I thought you was holdin' out on me. But I see now I was wrong."

"Don't give it a thought, Carmine. I can understand you thinkin' that. And I don't hold no grudge." He grinned. "In fact, I got even more for you. Remember that deal I said was coming up?"

Bill Knott

Caesar came out of the kitchen with Carmine's drink. Carmine took it from Caesar without thanking him and took a quick belt.

"What deal?"

"Four keys of near pure stuff."

"Jesus, Frank. Four keys? Where are they?"

"Downstairs right now. A repo man has it and he's waiting to deal."

Carmine frowned. "A repo man?"

"And he's willing to deal, more like an exchange, actually."

"For what?"

"For that Lamborghini I gave the cunt."

"Now wait a minute. Where'd this repo man get the stuff in the first place?"

"From her. The bitch was going into business for herself."

Carmine frowned. "That's a very ambitious lady you got there. I hope you stepped on her good."

"Hey, what do you think, Carmine? I know how to handle quiff like that."

"Okay. It don't matter how you handle it, Frank. Just so you do. Just don't get me involved. You sure this car is all the repo man wants?"

"That's what he says."

"You got the car to deal?"

"Sure." Frank paused. "Well, it's Luigi who's got it. He's hid it someplace."

"So how you goin' to get them four keys?"

"I'm going to take it from the silly bastard. What do you think?"

"That could be dangerous."

"Not for Caesar here."

Carmine glanced over at Caesar, then looked back at the money and took another belt of his drink.

"Frank, maybe I been selling you short. Right now, I like the way you think. But no cops. I can't afford that, Frank. You know the shit I got waitin' for me back in Jersey."

"No sweat, Frank. I own these town cops. Believe me, they come cheap. And don't worry about this fink downstairs. He's a nothin', a goddamn repo man way out on a limb."

Carmine nodded, satisfied. "So go on downstairs and make the deal. I might come in later. How's the fettuccine?"

"Hey, Carmine, it's the house specialty."

"I asked you how it was."

Frank shrugged unhappily. "Carmine, what can I say? This ain't Little Italy, right? You have to do the best you can with the talent you got. It'll get by. Try it, you'll like it."

He grinned at Carmine.

Carmine finished his drink, then walked over to the Formica table and snapped shut the attaché case.

"I'll just take this down to Gus," he told Frank.

He pushed aside the sliding doors and disappeared down the steps.

CHAPTER 13

"Do you think Mr. Santorini could have forgotten us?" Terry asked Skip.

She had put away most of the fettuccine Alfredo, and pushing the platter aside, took up her glass of wine.

"I been thinking, Terry. When Larry gets here, it'd be nice if you could keep him from coming on too soon."

"How do you propose I do that?"

"Stay with me until you've witnessed Santorini check out the contraband and consent to the deal.

Bill Knott

Then excuse yourself to powder your nose and stay out in the lobby to head him off."

"When should I bring him on?"

"Keep an eye on me. I'll beckon to you clear enough."

"You think you can do that without Santorini getting wise?"

"Didn't you know I used to be a cop?"

"A cop, yes. A narcotics agent, no."

"Hey, I was used in a narcotics stakeout once." He grinned at her. "I really learned a whole lot."

"I'm sure."

Frank Santorini pushed through the swing doors and came to a halt beside their booth, his eyes slipping quickly from Skip to Terry.

"Hey, now," he said, "and who's this lovely lady with Mr. Repo Man?" He looked back at Skip. "You goin' to introduce us or not?"

"Terry, meet Mr. Santorini. He runs this restaurant."

"And a whole lot more, I'll bet," said Terry, smiling at Santorini with dazzling effect.

Skip could see that Santorini was quite taken with Terry and that her presence had altered Santorini's opinion of him. In Terry's resplendent company he could not be viewed entirely as a fool.

"Sit down," Skip told Santorini. "We got business to discuss."

Santorini tried to fit in beside Skip's hard bulk, but quickly stood back up.

"Not enough room there," he said. "Wait a minute."

BODY PARTS

He gestured to a waitress, indicating he wanted a chair. It was swiftly brought over and Santorini sat down facing the end of the table, partially blocking the passage to and from the kitchen; but he was the boss, so that didn't bother him any. A moment later the zip who had tailed Skip to the restaurant pushed through the kitchen doors and sat down at a small empty table against the wall, his cold expressionless eyes fixed on Skip.

"How'd you like the fettuccine?" Santorini asked Terry.

"It was delicious," she said.

"I've tasted better," Skip said. "There's a little Italian restaurant on Depot Street, Albany, that has a very fine chef; his fettuccine Alfredo is a lot silkier. The cheese is better, too."

"Maybe we'll bring that chef up here," Santorini said. "Is he Italian?"

"No. Chinese."

Terry giggled.

The amiability left Santorini's face. "I see you got the goods," he said, glancing at the suitcase on the seat beside Skip.

"That's right. So where's the Lamborghini?"

"Let's see what you got in there first."

"Sure."

Skip snapped open the suitcase, reached into it, grabbed the Baggie on top and brought it out, slapping it down on the table in front of Santorini."

"Jesus!" Santorini said, looking quickly around as he snatched the Baggie and dropped it quickly down onto his lap. "Not out in plain sight! Don't you know nothin'? Whatsa matter with you?"

Skip shrugged. "I'm new in this business."

"Amateurs. Goddamn amateurs," Santorini muttered, untwisting the plastic tie sealing the Baggie.

"You talk like that," Skip told him, "and you might hurt my feelings."

Santorini moistened his forefinger and poked it into the cocaine. He withdrew it and flicked it with his tongue. His eyebrows lifted a notch.

"Well?" Skip asked.

"It's good stuff, all right. No shit."

"So where's the Lamborghini?"

"I don't have it."

"What do you mean, you don't have it? Where is it?"

"We got rid of it. Right now it's underwater somewhere. Forget about the car. We can deal without it."

Skip reached over deftly, grabbed the Baggie, slammed it back into the suitcase and clicked it shut.

"No Lamborghini, no cocaine," he pronounced loudly.

"Hey, keep your voice down," Santorini said, glancing nervously about him again. "Jesus."

"I wish you'd stop saying that," Terry said. "I'm a devout Catholic."

Startled, Santorini looked at her, then back at Skip.

For the moment there was a standoff. When Skip took back the Baggie, the zip had jumped to his feet, and Skip knew he was crazy enough to blast away; but a quick shake of Santorini's head sat him promptly back down. Meanwhile, a man Skip immediately recognized had brushed aside the hostess and entered the dining room. He walked heavily toward them, nodded almost imperceptively to Santorini, then carefully lowered his bulk into a chair at the zip's table.

He was Carmine DiAngelo, a prime mob figure. As a result of an ongoing RICO investigation, his face had been plastered over the New Jersey and New York papers almost daily during the past months. For a year now the grand jury had been digging into his mob connections. So far, DiAngelo was ahead. No indictments were in sight, and two members of the grand jury had disappeared. A third had died of natural causes, and a federal prosecutor had been found floating faceup in the Gowanus Canal.

"All right," Skip said with apparent reluctance. "You don't have the car, Santorini. But you say we can still deal?"

"Sure. Why not?"

"All right. I'll forget the car. It's no skin off my nose. How much you willing to give me for this stuff?"

Santorini moistened his lips. "Ten thousand?"

"For four *kilos?* You must be out of your head!"

"All right, give me a figure."

"I want at least double that. Twenty thousand."

"Fifteen."

"Eighteen."

"Sixteen."

"Done."

Watching Santorini, Skip could see the man was

having a very difficult time keeping a straight face. That Skip was asking only sixteen thousand dollars for four kilos of such high quality snow was to him incredible. The street value had to be close to half a million. In Santorini's eyes, Skip had to be suffering from a severe case of rectal darkness.

"Wait here," Santorini said.

He got up and walked over to DiAngelo. The don frowned, uneasy at being brought into this so openly; but he listened closely as Santorini told him how much Skip wanted for the four keys. DiAngelo glanced in surprise at Skip, then looked back at Santorini and nodded vigorously. Santorini spoke quietly to the zip, who got up and pushed through the swing doors into the kitchen.

Approaching the limo, Caesar was not surprised to see Gus reading a book in the soft glow of the limo's dome light. He rapped on the window. Gus put the book down and touched a small lever in the door. The window slid down.

"Hi, Caesar," Gus said. "How you been?"

"I been all right, Gus. Frank sent me out for sixteen grand. The don say it's all right. He say take it out of that case he just brought down."

"I don't know, Caesar. I think maybe I ought to get it straight from Carmine. That ain't my money, don't forget."

"You sayin' I can't be trusted?"

Gus smiled, a big, warm smile that Caesar knew

could turn mean fast. "You know better than that, Caesar. Just go on back inside and get a note from the don."

"Listen, Frank's got a deal on. It won't wait. The mark might get suspicious. Cut the shit and give me the money."

Gus didn't like his tone. Caesar had not expected him to. He hated this ass-sucking bastard as much as he hated his boss. He had seen this one smiling when the don chewed him out once, calling him a crazy Sicilian, a stupid peasant. Caesar pulled his .22 automatic out of his side pocket. He had already screwed the silencer into its barrel. As he lifted the weapon, Gus hit the window button. Caesar stuck the long silencer barrel in over the rising glass and pulled the trigger. There was a dull *pat*. The .22 slug planted a small black hole in Gus's temple. Gus slumped over onto his right side and the window stopped rising.

Caesar withdrew the .22 and tried the door. It was not locked. He opened it, pushed Gus over on the seat, pulled his body upright, then tugged the chauffeur's cap down over Gus's forehead. He reached over the seat and grabbed the attaché case. He set it down on the front seat between the upright dead man and himself, opened it, counted out the sixteen grand Frank wanted, took an extra grand for himself, then closed the case and flung it back onto the rear seat. He slipped the keys out of the ignition and turned off the dome light, then stepped out of the car and locked it.

Before he started back into the restaurant, he

peered through the side window. Gus's body was still upright on the seat, his head leaning back against it, his cap down over his eyes. Anyone passing the limo would think he was asleep.

───

Skip saw the zip step through the swing doors. Santorini got up from the booth and edged the zip back into the kitchen. A moment later the two of them returned. The zip sat back down at the table with DiAngelo. Santorini rejoined Skip and Terry, then slipped a wad of bills under the table to Skip.

With a wink at Terry, Skip brought the money up onto the table and counted it, after which he folded the wad once and dropped it into his jacket pocket. Then he lifted the overnight bag onto the table and slid it over to Santorini.

"Here you are, Mr. Santorini," Skip said. "It's been a pleasure doing business with you."

"Sure, sure," said Santorini, opening the case and poking through it until he saw the other sugar-filled Baggies Skip had placed under Mary Lou's things. Satisfied, he snapped the cover down and passed the case across the aisle to the zip, who slipped it between his chair and the wall.

Terry excused herself, muttering something about powdering her nose. Santorini watched her go, his eyes greedy, then looked back at Skip.

"Well," Skip said. "I guess I'll be pulling out."

"What's the hurry, friend?" Santorini asked.

As he spoke he glanced sidelong at the zip, who

BODY PARTS

sat up alertly. As Skip had guessed, Santorini had no intention of letting him walk out of here with his new fortune.

Just then Captain Larry Carmody, resplendent in his New York State Trooper's uniform, appeared in the dining room entrance. Within seconds he had spotted Skip. Terry was behind Carmody in the lobby, hurrying to overtake him. She called to him. Carmody glanced back at her, greeted her with a quick wave and brushed past the hostess. As big as life and twice as proud, Captain Larry Carmody marched straight for Skip's table.

At sight of the approaching trooper, Carmine DiAngelo left his chair and moved back out of the restaurant with astonishing swiftness and agility for a man of his size. The zip swore softly in Italian and vanished through the kitchen doors. The moment Skip saw Carmody approaching, he palmed the serrated bread knife and hooked one arm over Santorini's neck to hold him in place.

"Stay put, Frank," he said, pressing the blade's needle-sharp point into his side, deep enough to draw blood.

Oblivious to DiAngelo and the zip's swift exit, Carmody swept off his trooper's hat and halted in front of the table. Behind him, Terry was still hurrying to overtake him.

"Hi, Captain," Skip said. "Glad you could join us."

"Terry called me," Carmody told him, all business. "She said you had something for me."

"Yeah, that's right," Skip said. "The murder weapon. But right now I'd like to introduce you to

Bill Knott

Frank Santorini. He just purchased four kilos of a controlled substance from me. With Terry as a witness."

Carmody wasn't quick enough to stop Santorini as the desperate man twisted wildly out of Skip's grasp and lunged past him. He had almost reached the lounge entrance when Skip overtook him. The two went down heavily in an explosion of silverware and broken glass. Santorini's forehead struck the corner of the counter holding the cash register.

Dazed, he groaned softly, making no effort to break free of Skip's grasp. Behind them, two women were sprawled amidst a wreckage of tables and chairs. Combined with the other diners' shouts, their steady, high-pitched screams caused the walls to reverberate like a drum. Skip glanced up to see the lounge's patrons, drinks in hand, crowding through the beaded curtain to stare down at him and Santorini.

But he did not see Moon, and that was a relief. Where the hell was he?

Inside the limo Caesar snatched off Gus's cap and, with his right foot, kicked the dead man off the front seat onto the floor. He tugged the chauffeur's cap down snugly onto his own head, found it a little large for him, but decided it would have to do. Starting the limo, he slipped it into drive, tromped on the accelerator and cranked the wheel sharply to the

BODY PARTS

right. The Lincoln's formidable power astonished him as it spun the rear tires, flinging back a hail of gravel. The car slewed wildly, forcing Caesar to correct it hastily as he drove back around the restaurant to the parking lot in front. Gunning the car through the parked cars, he saw DiAngelo, arms waving frantically, dashing toward him. In the glare of the Lincoln's headlights Carmine could not see Caesar's face behind the wheel. Caesar stood on the brake pedal and skidded to a halt just beyond Carmine. Puffing like a steam engine, DiAngelo overtook the car, pulled open the rear door and flung himself inside.

"Good thinking, Gus," he wheezed, slamming the door shut. "Now, get us the hell out of here!"

Caesar gunned the motor and swept out of the parking lot. Accelerating smoothly, the Lincoln swept up Greentree Road. Guessing, Caesar cut right when he left it. It was dark now, and when he had driven into Lake Placid earlier, it had been daylight, so he was not certain he knew the way out of town. The Lincoln's powerful beams caught a sign ahead of him. In bright white letters it said Northway, with an arrow pointing to the intersection ahead. Caesar smiled and relaxed. He knew the way now.

He glanced in the rearview mirror. DiAngelo was resting back on his seat, still wheezing heavily, his eyes closed. About ten miles down the Northway, Caesar heard Carmine's heavy bulk shifting and he glanced at the rearview mirror. Carmine was sitting up, staring intently at the back of Caesar's head.

"Hey!" Carmine cried. "You ain't Gus! Who are you? Where are you taking me?"

Smiling, Caesar slowed and pulled to a halt on the shoulder. Then he picked the .22 automatic up off the seat beside him and turned around in his seat, shoving the silencer's muzzle into Carmine's face.

"Hello, Mr. DiAngelo."

"Caesar! My God, Caesar! This is crazy. Put away that gun."

"How you like this, huh? How you like to feel death pointing at you?"

"Goddammit, Caesar, you should be grateful! I'm the one called off that contract."

"It was Frank made you do it."

"What's the difference? I did it."

"I don't trust you, Mr. DiAngelo. You bring me over here and then you dump me."

"Enough of this, Caesar. Put away that pea shooter. And where's Gus?"

"You want to see Gus?"

"Of course I do."

"He's waiting in hell for you. Go see him."

Caesar pulled the trigger twice, planting one clean hole in DiAngelo's forehead and another in his starched white shirt over the sternum. Carmine settled loosely back in his seat, then slumped to one side.

Turning back around, Caesar pulled out onto the highway and kept going south, alert for a place to dump the two bodies. About twenty miles farther on he found a likely spot on a causeway that carried the interstate over a gorge. He pulled onto the

BODY PARTS

asphalt shoulder just beyond the causeway and halted close to the guardrail, got out and looked over the rail. The gorge was as black as the mouth of hell.

He opened the door on the passenger side and pulled Gus out of the car, dragged his body close to the guardrail and left it there, then returned to the limo for Carmine's body. He was opening the rear door when a highway patrol car, roof beacons flashing, pulled to a halt just behind the limo.

"What's the problem?" the trooper asked, his voice eager, friendly. "Out of gas?"

As trooper Martin cut in front of his patrol car, he caught a glimpse of a body sprawled facedown on the asphalt strip close by the guardrail. He looked up and saw a little man in a chauffeur's cap aiming a gun at him. The gun spat softly. The trooper felt something like a bee sting in his left shoulder.

He drew his magnum, went down on one knee and squeezed off three quick shots. He almost enjoyed the sight of the little man bucking with the impact of each bullet, then falling backward, his toy of a gun clattering to the pavement.

Aware of a growing, fearsome ache in his shoulder, the trooper walked over to the little man. He was dead. So was the man on the ground near the guardrail. Turning back to the limo, he opened its rear door wider and looked inside. In the garish strobe light of his patrol car's roof beacons, he had little difficulty recognizing the man slumped back against the seat.

The New Jersey mobster. Carmine DiAngelo.

"Holy Jesus," the trooper said, then reached out to grab the limo's roof as he realized he was a wounded man himself.

CHAPTER 14

Skip stood with Terry and Carmody in the restaurant's empty parking lot and watched as a trooper, one hand holding Frank Santorini's head down, shoved the handcuffed figure into the backseat of his blue-and-gold.

As the patrol car left, Carmody turned to Skip. "You said something about more cocaine."

"Three kilos, at least. I left it back in the motel safe. We can go after it later."

"You understand, Tracewski. There's not much likelihood this will hold up in court."

"Nothin' much does," Skip conceded.

"Even with my testimony?" Terry asked.

"It's all very shaky," Carmody explained. "I'm sure Santorini's attorney will call it entrapment. He'll say we tricked Santorini, enticed him."

Terry was incensed. "And of course we shouldn't do that to a drug dealer, right?"

"I don't make the laws, Terry."

"Well, at least it'll keep the son of a bitch on ice for a while," Skip said, "while we tie him into Jimmy Vasquez's murder."

Carmody addressed Skip like a schoolteacher would a not very bright student. "Tracewski, I know you were an Albany cop once, but this is my investigation, not yours. You collect cars. In the future, I suggest you restrict your activities to that specialty."

Skip grinned at the captain. "You don't want my help, then."

"Larry, I told you," Terry said urgently, "Skip knows where the murder weapon is."

"I understand that, Terry. That's why I'm here." He looked back at Skip. "All right, Tracewski. Where is it?"

"I only collect cars. Remember? I better not tell you."

Without batting an eye Carmody replied, "In that case, I would be forced to construe this as withholding evidence."

"Golly, I sure wouldn't want you to construe that."

"Will you two *stop* this!" Terry demanded.

Skip smiled at her. "All right, Terry. All right." He placed a reassuring hand on her arm and looked back at Carmody. "The ax is at Howie Randall's place."

"Randall? Who's he?"

"He works for Santorini—he's the bouncer here. He's got a place a few miles past Carlton. Do you know the town?"

"Of course."

"All right. Let's go, then."

Carmody hesitated. "I don't know if I can allow that."

Skip knew why. Regulations were pretty strict about passengers riding in a state patrol car. It had to do with liability.

"Larry," Terry said urgently, "we're wasting time. Don't you *want* that ax?"

That ended the discussion. Skip and Terry piled into the backseat. Carmody put his blue-and-gold in gear and drove out of the parking lot. Twenty minutes later, as they approached Carlton, Skip leaned forward and tapped Carmody on the shoulder.

"There's a Timberline Tavern this side of the bridge, Captain. Pull up when you get there. I've got to make a phone call."

Skip saw Carmody's neck stiffen at this imposition, but he showed admirable restraint, and a few minutes later pulled to a halt in front of the tavern. Skip got out, entered the tavern, found a pay phone on the wall beside the bar and dialed the number of the Maple Street Mobil in Saranac Lake.

"Yeah?"

"Is this Mel Dannenhower?"

"Yep."

Bill Knott

"This is Skip Tracewski. Mohawk Adjustment out of Albany. My brother Buford said you've worked for the agency before."

"Sure, I remember Buford."

"You mind working late tonight?"

"Not if the price is right."

"We'll see it is. Your wrecker healthy?"

"Healthy enough."

"Better bring some metal mats. You'll need them. The car we want is in some soft muck deep in the woods."

"Where's it located?"

"About five miles north of Carlton, off a logging road."

"I might have trouble finding it in the dark. Can you put some markers down?"

"I'll do better than that. I'll have a blue-and-gold, roof beacons flashing, at the entrance to the road."

"That ought to do it. I'll start right away."

Skip hung up, then called Buford and told him to have someone drive a flatbed up to the Thunderbird Motel in Lake Placid and wait for him there.

He left the tavern—and the silent, nervous patrons watching the black-and-gold sitting in the parking lot.

At first, lying on her back on the single bed, her wrists and arms tied to the bed's four corners, Carlotta had tried desperately to believe this could not really be happening to her.

BODY PARTS

Moon's capacity for sex was appalling. Already she was so sore down there she could feel it throbbing. Her stomach and rib cage ached where Moon had flung his powerful body down onto her. And as he grunted and howled and she felt his unshaven face rasping against her cheeks, she knew she was being punished, paid back for her lustful pursuit of Frank Santorini.

From the very beginning she had known he was Italian, but she'd seen the Godfather movie and had found herself fascinated by their violent sensuality, their fierce tribal loyalty, their fiery temperament. In marrying Frank, she had hoped for that same sensuality and lust she had seen portrayed on the screen and which she dared contemplate only in her wildest dreams. And, God help her, she had not been disappointed. In Frank's arms she found the forbidden delights she had craved secretly all her life. She had known it was wicked, but that had made no difference. Soon Frank's lovemaking was all she could think of—all she wanted. She had heard the phrase "a slave to desire," and now she knew exactly what that meant.

She saw now that all she had been was Frank Santorini's rich whore.

Moon had just pushed back off her and was slumped in his rocker, slurping at a can of Carlings beer, a growing pile of discarded beer cans on the floor around him. An unshaded floor lamp behind him provided the only light in the room. The naked bulb emitted a glare so harsh she was forced to squint as she peered past her naked body at Moon.

Bill Knott

When she had continued to protest shrilly his violation of her earlier, he had shoved a filthy sock into her mouth. It was still there, forcing her to concentrate all the hate and revulsion she felt for him into her gaze—which Moon now returned foggily.

She had managed to work the loathsome gag to the front of her mouth and could breathe easier. Once she managed to free her hands, she would spit it out. For now, however, she was content to leave it in her mouth, fearful of the use Moon would again make of her if it were gone.

Moon's lidded eyes closed, his chin sagging forward onto his massive chest.

Was he asleep?

She waited a moment longer, squinting at him through the glare of the light bulb. When she saw his hairy chest's steady, regular lift, she knew he was asleep. Irrational hope flooded her. She began tugging frantically on the ropes binding her wrists to the bedpost.

Then she saw the Doberman and all hope left her.

Moon had long since let the dog out of the bedroom, and now the hellish hound had just moved into her line of sight as it passed close under the windows behind Moon. It paid no attention to her, but she knew Moon had already spoken to it, commanding it not to let her out of the house. The guard dog would obey him through fire and flood, she realized. A few hours ago, as its master forced her to perform a particularly revolting act of perversion—one she had denied even Frank—this hellish brute had stopped by the bed to peer at her, tongue lolling,

BODY PARTS

eyes gleaming, as if it, too, were participating in the bestial act.

The dog was standing perfectly still now, its nose lifted toward the window. It began to whine.

Moon came awake at once and looked around at the dog. "Hey, Devil, who's out there, boy?"

The animal's perfectly molded body remained frozen while it continued to whine, its nose lifting in the direction of the danger it sensed in the yard below. Pulling on his Levi's, Moon got to his feet and turned off the light.

"Someone out there?" he asked the dog. He went to the window and peered out into the darkness. "I didn't hear no car drive up."

The dog's whining grew in intensity, and Moon reached for the shotgun leaning against the wall. He took out two cartridges from an open box on the windowsill, broke open the shotgun and loaded it, then snapped the weapon shut.

"Let's go," he said to the Doberman as he headed for the door.

Before he opened it, he snapped on the yard light. He had not even bothered to look back at Carlotta; as soon as he shut the door behind him, she spat out the gag and resumed her frantic tugging on the ropes that bound her.

A few minutes earlier Ahmed had driven past Moon's driveway. At Mary Lou's insistence he turned around on the narrow road and edged the van off it into a clump of pines.

"Can't you drive in deeper?" Mary Lou asked.

"This is far enough," Ahmed told her, peering out the side window through a pine branch spread flat against it. "We'll never get out of here if we go in farther."

"I just don't want no one to see us parked here."

"Who's goin' to see us? This here's the other side of the moon."

"Moon might see us."

"You're crazy. He's in town, working at Frank's."

"When we drove past the driveway, I saw a car parked there. And lights were on in the house. Moon might be in there."

"Well, shit, that's just fine. Give me a chance to pay that mother back."

"Don't talk crazy," Mary Lou said, opening the van's door and pushing out against the branches. "We only came here for one reason. The money."

She squeezed out of the van and closed the door softly behind her. Ahmed met her on the dirt road.

"You can wait here if you want," Mary Lou told him.

"I ain't afraid of that cracker."

When they reached the head of Moon's driveway, they ducked across it and into a tangle of brush on the far side. Mary Lou was right. There was a car parked close in under the deck, and what looked like an unshaded light was glowing in the front room.

"That's not Moon's car," Ahmed said.

"I know."

BODY PARTS

"It belongs to Carlotta, Frank's wife. What's she doin' up here?"

"Maybe she's got something goin' with Moon."

"Could he be *that* good?"

"He sure could. You ever hear of a perpetual motion machine? Frank's got nothin' on him."

"Now, how would you know that?"

In the darkness he saw her teeth flash as she smiled at him.

"You mean you . . . and Moon . . . ?"

She shrugged. "He's got as much right as anyone."

"And then you let him beat on you like a bongo drum?"

"He didn't have nothin' to say about it, Ahmed. That was Frank's idea."

"C'mon, let's grab the money and get the fuck out of here."

Mary Lou led the way through the brush toward the barn. Unseen branches slapped at their faces, and they stumbled repeatedly over weed-covered boulders embedded in the ground. Cursing under his breath, Ahmed was furious with himself for not thinking to bring his flashlight. They reached the barn and Ahmed halted. With part of its roof missing and a gaping hole in the back, it looked straight out of *Friday the Thirteenth*.

Edging inside the barn, Mary Lou said, "The money's in a beach bag. I came out one night and hid it when Moon went to sleep on me."

"Where?"

"Near the corner, under a loose board."

"Should be a cinch."

Bill Knott

"It would be if it wasn't so dark."

"Want me to go back for a flashlight?"

"No. If Moon's home, he'll see the light."

"So we grope around in the dark."

"Just head for that corner."

She pushed ahead of him, Ahmed following after her. She kept low, but he was walking upright and his forehead slammed suddenly into a huge, unyielding hunk of metal hanging from a rafter. It was so heavy it didn't move an inch when he struck it. He sagged to the barn's floor, clutching his head. He could feel the blood flowing from a break in his scalp.

"Oh, I should've told you about that," Mary Lou said, crawling swiftly to his side.

"What the fuck *is* that?" Ahmed asked.

"An engine block Moon's working on. It's hanging from a rafter."

"Find the fucking money, will you," Ahmed pleaded, "so we can get the fuck out of here."

"I'm not sure exactly which board it's under, Ahmed. It was dark when I hid it."

"Just get it!"

A powerful porch light snapped on, flooding the yard with a near daytime brilliance. One shaft of light entering through a missing board in the side of the barn highlighted the dismantled engine suspended over Ahmed's head as well as a good deal of the barn's interior. Immediately they heard someone descending the steps.

"Oh, Jesus," said Ahmed. "Here comes the bastard!"

BODY PARTS

"Ahmed," Mary Lou said in a small voice. "Moon has a dog."

"A dog? What kind?"

"A Doberman."

"Forget the money. We're splittin'!"

"Look! Over there! Under that loose board. I can see it!"

As Mary Lou moved toward the now visible beach bag, Ahmed caught sight of a pitchfork leaning against a wall. He scrambled to his feet and grabbed it just as Moon's Doberman bounded into the barn. Instinctively, Ahmed lifted the rusted tines to shield himself. A vicious growl coming from deep in its throat, the Doberman sprang, impaling itself on the pitchfork. One crooked tine penetrated a nostril but did not go deep, while the rest slipped into its throat. The Doberman yelped piteously but kept struggling to get at him anyway. Ahmed braced himself and kept the pressure on the tines, letting the Doberman's frantic lunging send the tines in still deeper. A dark gout of blood spurted from its neck. With a despairing yelp, it flopped over on its side, its teeth bared, its tail flopping on the floorboards.

"Ahmed!" Mary Lou cried, dashing past him out of the barn, the beach bag in her hand. "I got it! Come on!"

Before Ahmed could follow after her, Moon appeared in the doorway through which the Doberman had bounded, a double-barreled shotgun in his hand. Ahmed turned and dashed after Mary Lou. He was out of the barn, caught in the full glare of the yard light, when he heard the blast behind him and felt the hot sting of buckshot punch into his lower back. He was lifted violently, then flung brutally to the ground.

Turning into the driveway, Carmody saw what was going on and hit the siren and roof beacons. Cutting sharply to avoid the sprawling black man Moon had just shot down, Carmody drove straight toward the barn and the huge hulk of a man caught in his high beams, a shotgun still raised to his shoulder.

"Duck," cried Skip, pushing Terry to the floor and throwing himself on top of her. "He's going to use that!"

The shotgun detonated. The buckshot shattered the windshield, blasting a jagged hole through it. Most of the charge expended itself on the front seat. With a cry, Carmody flung his hand up to his face as the car crunched to a halt against the barn's corner post.

Skip pushed open the door and threw himself out of the car. Moon was clearly visible in the patrol car's beams as he yanked a pitchfork out of his fallen Doberman and started for Skip. At the same time, Skip saw the ax behind Moon. Someone had lifted and flung away the board covering it. As Moon started for him with the pitchfork, Skip ducked past him and snatched up the ax.

When he turned with it, Moon rushed him. Skip jumped aside as Moon hurled the pitchfork at him. The pitchfork missed, its tines sinking deep into the

BODY PARTS

rotted floorboards. Skip swung the ax. It missed Moon by a foot. Moon then snatched up a fallen beam longer than the ax and clubbed Skip in the midsection. Skip doubled over. Moon struck him again in the side, causing Skip to drop the ax and fall to the floor. Groggily, Skip looked up to see Moon towering over him. He had snatched up the ax and was swinging it up over his head.

A shot came from the car. Moon staggered, but remained upright. Skip rolled quickly aside. A second shot came and then another. Moon dropped the ax, turned, and saw Terry standing next to the patrol car's open door, Carmody's .357 magnum in her hands. He sank to his knees and pitched forward.

Skip got slowly to his feet. He ached something awful. "Thanks, Terry," he managed.

"Is . . . is that the ax?"

"That's it."

"I won't ask how it got there."

"Thanks."

"Carmody's hurt, his right cheek."

"Call for backup, I'll see to that one over there on the ground."

She nodded, her face drawn. She had performed well. He was proud of her—and very, very grateful.

A woman up in Moon's house began screaming then: short, panicky cries that froze them both. Terry looked at Skip for explanation. That was when he spotted Carlotta's car parked under the deck.

"Carlotta, I think. Santorini's wife. That ape you just shot must've been keeping her up there."

"Oh, my God, Skip."

Bill Knott

"Maybe you better be the first to see her."

Skip left the barn and examined Ahmed. He was cut nearly in half by Moon's shotgun blast. He was still alive, though, twisting slowly on the ground like a cut worm. A motor roared to life in the road. Skip glanced up and saw Ahmed's van charging past the driveway, Mary Lou bent over the wheel. He looked to see if Terry had noticed. She was in the blue-and-gold's front seat beside Carmody, her head bent over the mike as she called in for backup. When he turned back to Ahmed, he saw he was no longer moving.

Carlotta was still screaming.

With his chin swathed in bandages, Carmody stood beside Terry. Two more troopers had joined them and were standing behind Terry and Carmody. Skip knocked loudly on the Ford's trunk.

"You still in there, Luigi?"

"Get me out of here, you bastard!" came the muffled cry.

"Tell me again. Were you working for Frank Santorini when you and Moon went to that motel after Mary Lou?"

"Yes! Let me outta here, for Christ sake!"

"And you saw Moon use that ax to whack out the kid?"

"You bastard, I already told you I saw it."

"Why didn't you help the kid?"

"You nuts? No one could've stopped that crazy bastard. Hey, for Christ sake, get me out of here!"

"Can't. Someone locked the keys in the trunk."

Skip stepped away from the car and nodded to Mel Dannenhower. The owner of the Maple Street Mobil advanced to the trunk, wedged a wrecking bar in under the lid and with one deft thrust sprang the lock. He lifted the lid and stepped back as Luigi sat up, stinking in his own excrement, blinking at the troopers staring in at him.

"Ah, shit," he said.

CHAPTER 15

IT WAS A BRIGHT SATURDAY AFTERNOON, A WEEK AFTER that business in Lake Placid and the futility of it that Carmody had seen coming all the way. Someone had snatched the single bag of pure stuff Skip had placed in the overnight case, so all they found in it were Baggies filled with sugar. Santorini was going to walk. Skip was lucky Frank's lawyer didn't charge him with assault with a deadly bread knife. Luigi had not been read his Miranda rights, so his muffled statement from inside the car trunk was clearly inadmissable. But Skip could live with this. The psycho who had murdered Jimmy Vasquez was dead—

Bill Knott

and the dealer in Miami had his Lamborghini back. Buford could still stand by his boast, "We never fail."

Skip had not seen Terry all week. She had called earlier in the day to ask if he wanted to drive her out to look over the cabin again. Though he had no wish to do so, something in her voice had sobered him at once and he had agreed. This time, after going through it more thoroughly with Terry at his side, he hadn't found it quite so unsuitable. They were sitting now on the screened-in porch. He was leaning back in a yellow metal armchair, and Terry had brushed off a picnic-table bench and was sitting on it with her hands folded almost primly in her lap, gazing out over the lake.

She cleared her throat. "Well? What do you think?"

"Not so bad, at that," he admitted. "A nice spot."

"And wouldn't you say the price is right?"

"Right enough when you consider what has to be done."

"What would that be?"

"Needs a new roof for sure. You saw how the ridge pole is sagging. The plumbing in the kitchen is nearly rusted out. And the tiles from the septic tank'll have to be dug up and a new drain field put in. I guess that's enough for starters."

"I noticed some cracks in the foundation," she said softly.

"Yeah, that, too."

"And you'll have to rip up that cracked linoleum in the kitchen."

"That wouldn't be much of a job."

"Does that mean you're interested?"

"No, Terry," he told her. "Not really."

"You're sure of that, Skip?"

"I'm sure. This is a pleasant enough spot, but it's not for me."

"You prefer the motel."

"Like I said, it makes life a lot simpler."

Terry nodded sadly, as if she had expected this response from the beginning—and was free now to tell him the real reason she had brought him out here. But she was not ready for that right then, and returned her gaze to the lake, remaining silent.

To fill the silence, Skip found himself asking how Larry Carmody was.

"Much better," she responded quickly. "But he'll have some slight scarring on his cheek and neck, I'm afraid. Any plastic surgery would be too expensive and not really worth it."

"That's too bad."

"Not really. It's helped him see his way much clearer."

"What do you mean?"

"He's leaving the troopers, Skip. Taking a job in Washington."

"Washington D.C.?"

"Yes."

"How come?"

"He's going to be working in a very well-known think tank. Very up front. Very now. They're dealing with the whole range of socioeconomic problems of urban life. Larry's very excited at the prospect of being a part of it. It was his dissertation that caught their eye." She hesitated a moment, then rushed on. "He's sick of what he sees, Skip, everywhere around him. The people he has to deal with daily, the pure crud of society, and then the utter futility of it all. Law enforcement, he says, is like digging a hole in shit, while the shit keeps piling up. Eventually it'll drown us all."

"He sounds bitter."

"Well, wasn't that why you quit the Albany force, Skip?"

"Maybe it was."

"You *know* it was."

"And what about you, Terry?" he asked, his voice sounding hollow in his ears.

She turned, ready now, her eyes meeting his squarely. "I'm going with Larry, Skip."

"I see. To help him in that think tank?"

"Of course I'll help him, Skip. He respects my intelligence, just as I respect his. He makes me feel good about myself. But it's more than that."

"I know. You want a family."

"And a home. Does that sound so odd?"

"It sounds perfectly normal."

"I'm glad you see it that way, Skip. I knew you'd understand."

Speaking past the growing tightness in his throat, he said, "We better start back now. This time of day, the mosquitoes get real fierce."

Skip got to his feet. Tears gleamed in Terry's eyes as she walked with him to the screen door. He held it open for her. As she passed him—so close her

BODY PARTS

shoulder brushed his chest lightly—he wanted to take her in his arms and tell her that he did not want her to go to Washington D.C. with Larry Carmody. He wanted her to stay here with him.

Instead he said nothing and stepped carefully down the shaky wooden steps after Terry, letting her lead the way back up the slope to his car.

COME WALK THESE MEAN STREETS

AND FIND CHEAP LOWLIFE, BRUTAL MURDER...AND GREAT READING!

NEON FLAMINGO
Matt and Bonnie Taylor
Reporter Palmer Kingston knows a scoop when he smells it—and he smells plenty when a retired cop is murdered.
_____ 91622-1 $3.95 U.S./$4.95 Can.

A NICE LITTLE BEACH TOWN
E.C. Ward
An old fisherman kills himself in a quiet California town. Or so everyone but Chandler Cairns thinks. Chandler thinks it's murder—and soon, the killer's after *him*...
_____ 92230-2 $3.95 U.S./$4.95 Can.

CHAIN SAW
Jackson Gillis
Is Julie Mapes really the daughter of a deceased timber baron in Washington State? Or is it a con—or worse? Former cop Jonas Duncan is out to learn the truth.
_____ 92217-5 $3.95 U.S./$4.95 Can.

Publishers Book and Audio Mailing Service
P.O. Box 120159, Staten Island, NY 10312-0004

Please send me the book(s) I have checked above. I am enclosing $_____ (please add $1.25 for the first book, and $.25 for each additional book to cover postage and handling. Send check or money order only—no CODs.)

Name _____

Address _____

City _____ State/Zip _____

Please allow six weeks for delivery. Prices subject to change without notice. Payment in U.S. funds only. New York residents add applicable sales tax.

MEAN 5/90

THE MEASURE OF A MAN IS HOW WELL HE SURVIVES LIFE'S MEAN STREETS

BOLD NEW CRIME NOVELS BY TODAY'S HOTTEST TALENTS

CAJUN NIGHTS
D.J. Donaldson
A rash of weird, violent murders haunts New Orleans—and each new clue to the perpetrator leads investigator Kit Franklyn deeper into a world of bloody revenge.
_____ 91610-8 $3.95 U.S. _____ 91611-6 $4.95 Can.

MICHIGAN ROLL
Tom Kakonis
Four quirky—and very dangerous—strangers show up in Traverse City, Michigan. Seduction, drug-dealing, death—it's certainly more than gambler Timothy Waverly bargained for.
_____ 91684-1 $3.95 U.S. _____ 91686-8 $4.95 Can.

SUDDEN ICE
Jim Leeke
A lonely Ohio farmhouse goes up in flames, killing two...or so it seems. Then the county Sheriff learns the hapless couple were killed before the fire started...
_____ 91620-5 $3.95 U.S. _____ 91621-3 $4.95 Can.

Publishers Book and Audio Mailing Service
P.O. Box 120159, Staten Island, NY 10312-0004

Please send me the book(s) I have checked above. I am enclosing $_____
(please add $1.25 for the first book, and $.25 for each additional book to cover postage and handling. Send check or money order only—no CODs.)

Name _____

Address _____

City _____ State/Zip _____

Please allow six weeks for delivery. Prices subject to change without notice. Payment in U.S. funds only. New York residents add applicable sales tax.

M STREET 5/90

HEY! WHATZA MATTA WI'CHU? YOU BETTA READ MEAN STREETS OR YOU'RE GONNA PAY

DROP-OFF
Ken Grissom
All John Rodrique thought he had to do for the two grand was sink a boat. Then he learned nothing's that simple in the Gulf of Mexico...
_____ 91616-7 $3.95 U.S. _____ 91617-5 $4.95 Can.

BAD GUYS
Eugene Izzi
Jimbo Marino's earned the trust of the Mob. Not bad for an undercover cop. But now an old enemy's out of prison—and has a score to settle with Jimbo...
_____ 91493-8 $3.95 U.S. _____ 91494-6 $4.95 Can.

MEXICAN STANDOFF
Bruce Cook
Chico Cervantes' latest job sounded easy. Just cross the border into Mexico, grab a fugitive, and return. But then there's that dead cop on the floor of his hotel room...
_____ 92114-4 $3.95 U.S./$4.95 Can.

Publishers Book and Audio Mailing Service
P.O. Box 120159, Staten Island, NY 10312-0004

Please send me the book(s) I have checked above. I am enclosing $_____
(please add $1.25 for the first book, and $.25 for each additional book to cover postage and handling. Send check or money order only—no CODs.)

Name _____
Address _____
City _____ State/Zip _____

Please allow six weeks for delivery. Prices subject to change without notice. Payment in U.S. funds only. New York residents add applicable sales tax.

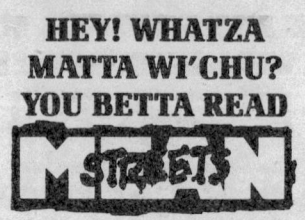

MEAN 2 5/90

YOU WANT IT?
YOU GOT IT!
MORE
MEAN STREETS

THE TOUGH NEW BREED OF CRIME NOVEL

A CALL FROM L.A.
Arthur Hansl
When his best buddy is cut down in a botched hit, Johnny Storm returns to his old haunts in Tinseltown to get to the bottom of it.
_____ 91618-3 $3.95 U.S. _____ 91619-1 $4.95 Can.

BLOOD UNDER THE BRIDGE
Bruce Zimmerman
When his lover is found brutally murdered, Quinn Parker is the prime suspect. To save himself, he must hunt down the madman responsible for this and a rash of other killings...
_____ 92244-2 $3.95 U.S. _____ 92245-0 $4.95 Can.

PEPPER PIKE
Les Roberts
Private dick Milan Jacovich is hired by a rich executive—then learns the man is killed hours later. Soon Jacovich finds himself enmeshed in the web of the Midwest Mob.
_____ 92213-2 $3.95 U.S./$4.95 Can.

Publishers Book and Audio Mailing Service
P.O. Box 120159, Staten Island, NY 10312-0004

Please send me the book(s) I have checked above. I am enclosing $_____
(please add $1.25 for the first book, and $.25 for each additional book to cover postage and handling. Send check or money order only—no COVs.)

Name _____
Address _____
City _____ State/Zip _____

Please allow six weeks for delivery. Prices subject to change without notice. Payment in U.S. funds only. New York residents add applicable sales tax.

MORE MS 5/90

TOUGH STREETS

The grit, the dirt, the cheap cost of life—the ongoing struggle between the law...and the lawbreakers.

BIG TIME TOMMY SLOANE
James Reardon
_____ 90981-0 $3.95 U.S. _____ 90982-9 $4.95 Can.

TIGHT CASE
Edward J. Hogan
_____ 91142-4 $3.95 U.S. _____ 91143-2 $4.95 Can.

RIDE A TIGER
Harold Livingston
_____ 90487-8 $4.95 U.S. _____ 90488-6 $5.95 Can.

THE RIGHT TO REMAIN SILENT
Charles Brandt
_____ 91381-8 $3.95 U.S. _____ 91382-6 $4.95 Can.

THE EIGHTH VICTIM
Eugene Izzi
_____ 91218-8 $3.95 U.S. _____ 91219-6 $4.95 Can.

THE TAKE
Eugene Izzi
_____ 91120-3 $3.50 U.S. _____ 91121-1 $4.50 Can.

Publishers Book and Audio Mailing Service
P.O. Box 120159, Staten Island, NY 10312-0004

Please send me the book(s) I have checked above. I am enclosing $_____
(please add $1.25 for the first book, and $.25 for each additional book to cover postage and handling. Send check or money order only—no CODs.)

Name _____

Address _____

City _____ State/Zip _____

Please allow six weeks for delivery. Prices subject to change without notice. Payment in U.S. funds only. New York residents add applicable sales tax.

TS 1/89